En.

CW00690686

A. L. I. S.

June
2024

Men of Seeking Arrangement

ALICE LONDON

Copyright © 2023. Alice London. All rights reserved.

No part of this publication may be reproduced, stored in a retrieval
system, or transmitted, in any form or by any means, electronic or
mechanical, including photocopy or recording, without the prior
permission in writing of the publisher, nor be otherwise circulated in any
form of binding or cover than that in which it is published and without
a similar condition including this condition being imposed on the
subsequent purchaser. If you would like to use material from the book,
prior written permission must be obtained by contacting
the author and the publisher.

This is a work of fiction. Names, characters, places, and incidents are
either the products of the author's imagination or are used fictitiously.
Any resemblance to actual persons, living or dead, events,
or locales is entirely coincidental.

Paperback ISBN# 979-8-9892269-0-0
Hardcover ISBN# 979-8-9892269-1-7
E-Book ISBN# 979-8-9892269-2-4

For women who choose to live their lives fiercely on their own terms. And to all the real men who are able to love women like that unconditionally.

Caute

Dating is the process of getting to know someone and may or may not lead to a relationship.

Relationship is a continuing committed association between two people, as in a family, friendship, marriage, partnership, or other interpersonal link in which the participants have some degree of influence on each other's thoughts, feelings, and actions.

Arrangement relationship regulating the amount of love that is able to flow; they are a place of convenience and comfort where we can keep ourselves hidden away to any extend we want. The arrangement can take its next step and start to evolve into a relationship.

Contents

CHAPTER 1

Change a Break Can Bring

"Separated could very well be married to a wife who knows nothing about his Seeking profile and occasional use of this apartment"

It had been a few weeks since she did it, and it felt like it had been years. It was one of those feelings when it is ongoing, it is fine, but once you take a break, it feels like you are starting over. It was uncomfortable.

She went online to recheck his profile and refresh the few details he chose to disclose about himself. Almost twice her age, beautiful and in shape, a decent number of millions worth, and separated. Separated was the main word here, the start of this game, where she guessed the lie and whether there was a slight chance she might have found an honest man—someone like her, pure in ways not many understood.

The drive to his place was easy; it was close enough, so it won't upset her if he didn't turn up. She parked on the curb by the side of the apartment building and stepped into the lobby. She texted him twice. No answer. She thought: *He was not real, and going to get groceries right now would make the most sense before returning home.*

Anticipation of the unknown was always a resentment. Five years of psychological research into who she really was completely transformed her, but some reactions had to be still worked on.

She decided to call him; he instantly picked up the phone call with a pleasant, welcoming voice. He did not get those last two texts. He apologized for keeping her waiting.

He walked toward her. He was beautiful. Everything was beautiful about him. Eyes with another different universe in them. Glowing moist skin. Lean athletic body. The energy he gave out was similar to what you would feel entering Disney World as an adult. You did not know what to expect, but you could see and feel something pleasant was about to happen.

Nothing alarming was about him except the place. He did not live there. No one lived there. It might have been some rental apartment in between renters, or it was his cheating grounds. Separated could be married to a wife who knows nothing about his Seeking profile and occasional use of this apartment.

Sparkling water in wine glasses, two plates with healthy takeout food from the restaurant on the side of the building. A brief exchange of travel destinations they had on Been apps. Twenty minutes later, they sat beside each other on the couch, and she gently played with his fingers. Nothing was missing, and it was unusual, almost weird. It was a given everyone she ever came close to felt like they knew her for years. It was the talent she polished and nurtured with love all her life. But she rarely felt the same. Could it be because these last few weeks of being alone changed her? Was it loneliness? Or maybe he was the one. Separated, mature, beautiful, self-sufficient man looking for an equal woman to start over. Or perhaps he was a married liar and cheater taking advantage of an available rental. The bedding had a scent of freshly cleaned sheets. His elevated body temperature gave out everything he was not saying out loud. He was waiting for her to make a move. And she waited. She enjoyed this anticipation of a possible love story, even if it was for an evening. It had been months since she felt anything similar to this. And she gave in.

His mouth felt like home. She could almost predict which turn his tongue is going to make next. His hands were demanding and gentle. He was everywhere she liked him to be and nowhere near anything she would say no to tonight.

Her mouth was wet, and she gave him almost all of it willingly; she had counted hundreds of kisses on his stomach. The skin on her face was on fire and burning. They were on fire, not one of those campfires you can do with your kids. It was a wildfire with the power to burn down acres of everything coming in between them in those few hours.

If it was not arranged and he had met her at the bar of his restaurant, this could have been a story to write a book about. But that book would have nothing new to offer to its readers. She was nothing like he ever came across. You could never meet her in the real world unless she arranged it herself.

CHAPTER 2

The Exciting New

"New was always exiting"

Three, almost four years of absolute freedom of choice, away from the dictatorship of the traditional world, constantly criticized or wowed by others, she lived an exceptional life filled with sacred dreams regular population called fantasies. Imagine the top 1% of this world's successful male population: wealthiest, most intelligent, famous, influential, untouchable. What would you give to have a glimpse of what is inside their head when no one is watching?

There was a time when meeting people on the street, Facebook, Instagram, Ashley Madison, and MillionareMatch did not provide her with anything she was after. She was after nothing less than exceptional and extraordinary male figures. Men have everything but time to connect with anyone on a human level. We are not talking about sex; we are talking about colliding two abnormally amazing strangers into one on all possible levels. Do you believe in magic? But did you know how mentally damaging magic spells can be with the magician who's done it all? What game does the player play when he is bored? He plays with open cards.

New was always exciting. She edited her Seeking profile for three weeks every day until it projected her whole character into three sentences. Ordinary men asked questions, and everyone wanted to know what she could do for them. And occasionally, one or two out of a hundred precisely did what she wanted. They complimented her three sentences.

His profile was simple and regular, and it was inviting. He was older, single, had a clear touristic picture showing his face and body type, and had over a million dollars yearly income with a hundred million net worth. That's it. No page-long self-description, zero requirements. He wrote her a short message that he was out of town traveling for the next three weeks, and he would hate to miss an opportunity to meet her by not being in town that day. They exchanged numbers, and she forgot about him.

Exactly three weeks later, she was driving on the day and time of her choice to a new restaurant that had just opened nearby his house. It was not the first time she had gone out to meet someone on an arranged date like that. Her very first date never showed. Few others were not the people from their profile pictures. Some wasted their time out of boredom and loneliness. Seeking free ears on a coffee break and seeking an arrangement is not the same. It was different that night, and she was nervous and scared of the exceptional unknown she had finally found.

She had a habit of arriving early. She parked as close as possible to the restaurant's entrance and waited to see if he also chose to arrive early. His made-to-order Ferrari made a sharp, confident turn five minutes before 7 pm. The driver chatted with the valet for a good minute and parked his car in front of the restaurant himself. Later she would see this bizarre picture over and over again for years. No one was allowed to park his cars. He was generous to a fault with everything in his life, but no other man could ever touch his cars or his women. He had many, but not many lasted.

He saw her getting out of her Mercedes and crossing the street.

After ten years of active modeling and numerous technics on how to walk beautifully she learned since she was twelve, she always turned heads, all heads. His head turned and froze at her coming close to him too. The look in his eyes was so confident; if she did not know better, she would think he scanned through her deepest thoughts when she stopped walking. Her nervousness and fear turned to inner panic.

She got people to love her by smiling and laughing, generously asking questions about their well-being, and spreading positivity. That night, she could not. She wanted to make it all great, and because that particular date was important to her, she acted the opposite of her regular self. The restaurant was too dark and too cold.

Food choices they both looked up for themselves from the restaurant's website before the date were not available that day. There was no lemon at an Asian fusion restaurant to add to her green tea. His life stories of beating his sister, him not being allowed back to his birth country for sponsoring rebels with guns to take down the ruling president, him threatening to shoot his ex-wife in front of their teenage children, and it went on. It would be best if you thought she was crazy to want to be with him after all those confessions. It did not matter to her. Somewhere deep inside, she was no better than him. And that did not matter to her too. For an hour and a half, she was the biggest unpleasant bitch to restraint's stuff and him. He did not say a word. His patience deserved the Nobel Price Award.

Nothing else could go wrong. It was over before it started. Pathetic. He walked her to her car, and she drove off after a brief friendly kiss on his cheek. The dark, cold hole she felt in her chest was deeper than space. There were no thoughts in her constantly multitasking head. What was it? What happened to her? Why could not she control herself? Did he notice she was nervous?

An hour after, he texted her: "I can't wait to see you again, and I hope you won't make me wait too long. You are gorgeous and need to be a little nicer to waiting personnel."

CHAPTER 3

I Want it, I Get it

*"You love yourself when you do only things you want to do
and never do anything you don't want to do"*

There is a thing people like to say to compliment someone who has done well for themselves. Most situations start with "You grew up as an amazing person" or "You became an example to all of us." She has proven to everyone that she can achieve greatness for thirty years. She can lead, inspire, and set an example to be that particular person. In a daily process of constant studying, analyzing, and improving, she got there. She achieved all her dreams one by one. Relatively fast, not necessarily easy. And a day came when a little quote popped up in her Instagram feed.

It was something like, "You don't become a leader; you are born a leader."

This simple sentence set up a reset button in her universe. She understood she no longer needed to try to be someone she was born as. Thirty years she spent on something unnecessary. It was the last day she lived for someone else's approval.

Do you know what it means to love yourself? People search for an answer to this question in different places, and only a few find it.

However, the answer is inside each one of you. You love yourself when you do things you want and never do anything you don't want to do. How long does it take to change your life into your everyday paradise? About two weeks.

And never again she gave a minute of her life to anyone she was not interested in herself. Her interests were simple. Her personal life was meant to happen only with people she liked. She wanted to be surrounded by exceptional men who were never bored, men who looked at the three sentences on her profile, and their life changed for a bit because spending time with her was not like anything they had ever felt.

His 8 a.m. morning dates were similar to what a mother feels taking her child on the second day of school in first grade.

She was rushing, never fully awake, and not being a morning person certainly did not help. He had to be out of the house by nine-fifteen, and she had to be there on time. Would that be strange if I told you she has never been late for anything? Not once. Not for a minute.

Passing the security gate and the front desk in his building was more complicated than international customs in some countries. She was taking her panties off in the elevator with two security cameras poised at her. His front door was always open before her arrival, and the moment she stepped inside, the version of your normal universe stopped existing.

Some mornings he loved her like he was running for the win at the Olympics. Passionately kissing her mouth while telling her how much he loved to be with her. He was asking her to go away with him. It was her favorite thing—the most normal traditional way of lovemaking. Bodies wrapped around, moving in unison hard and strong. No, she was not just lying under him; they were both in a race to reach the land of satisfaction. Only kissing in a missionary position made her feel small and vulnerable; she enjoyed and cherished the memories of it. It was someone she thought she would like to be, not who she was.

On other mornings he did not remember her name or how they met. Alarming, no? He would pin her to his massage table and tell her stories about his two official girlfriends, describing how much he likes to make them uncomfortable to share him in front of each other. She wondered how much weirder she would let it go to stop returning to him.

Some days they bought guns and discussed how to help people in need without breaking laws on the upcoming missionary trip overseas. It was always a drive twice above the speed limit on the highway. They had never needed a reservation or to wait for a table for dinner. Anywhere. He shared his life stories and business achievements—it was inspiring and surprising! He loved people, and there was no one in his life not wholly cared for. Some days he would shoot down dozens of beautiful African animals. Have you ever seen those pictures? She could not breathe when she had to look at how proud he was. He never overstepped her personal space. It was the perfect arrangement except for the occasional details he shared about his life and the exceedingly sick questions he asked during sex.

If Tony Montana had survived at the end of Scarface (1983) and made it to our time, he would be the Tony Montana of our time. She would gladly share all the scary stuff mentioned above, but she would need psychiatric help after reviving the details of some stories and questions. And you would need help too. So, let's leave it as is.

CHAPTER 4

Law of Attraction

*"On the surface this guy possesses all
the qualities of a dream guy"*

Sometimes you look at two people in a relationship and start to see a visual resemblance between them. They have similar facial features, and for the most part, they are friends, not lovers. Many years ago, she married a man who looked nothing like her, and they had never been friends or lovers. Male friends she had she was not particularly sexually or emotionally attracted to. Her lovers were either fully married and unavailable emotionally; or single and wanting to marry her since day one. None of that worked. It was boring, predictable, and too simple. She often wondered what it would feel to love someone with a similar outlook on life as her, constantly improving himself and being against anything ordinary, and one day he found her.

His profile belonged to an athletic thirty-nine-year-old mixed-race finance guy standing wonderfully beautifully shirtless in his photo on Ipanema beach in Rio. Single, no kids, overeducated, travel lots, love good food. She never cared about an outer beauty of a man. Never. She was purely sexually attracted to the intellect of her partner only. But that photo on Ipanema Beach was doing something strange to her.

Every third person contacting her on Seeking asked the same question: is she real? Explaining this like they never met a woman like her, and they have doubted her profile was authentic. Those men were not the men for her, and it was annoying that the same phenomenon happened repeatedly. And now, going over his profile, she understood it. On the surface, this guy possesses all the qualities of a dream guy. That naturally doesn't exist in real life! He was her! They were the same impossible kind.

Judging from the bar he chose to meet at, he was not local. Have you ever seen those gestures celebrities do for their loved ones, like renting a whole restaurant or a movie theatre or an attraction park to be with them alone? Well. She entered an absolutely empty bar at one of the most popular high-end touristic hotels during Art Basel. A beautiful man looking like an unborn child of a Will Smith and Jason Olive was typing something into his iPhone. This was the first and last time he had his phone in his hands for the twenty-six days they had spent together.

She is an exceptional conversationalist on any subject, and she did not talk much that evening. They walked a few blocks side by side on the wet old streets of the city. She was worried about the leather bottoms of her limited-edition Jimmy Choo heels, and he looked like he would gladly lift her up and never let her off him if she only asked. Three hours-long dinner at a pretty good Mediterranean restaurant flew by like fifteen minutes. He was incredible, like a real-life James Bond from some new variation of Marvel's Avengers. Imagine all the intelligent, interesting people we have on this planet. How many of them speak 14 languages fluently, hold top degrees from almost all-American educational institutes, explore 194 countries, and the list goes on.

All that knowledge is in one person! If you are wondering what was the last county on Earth his foot did not step in, it was Madagascar. There was no particular reason, and it was on his list once he returned to an area. With her 34 countries marked on her Been app, she felt like an intern at a major travel agency. When everything in that restaurant was tried and eaten, none of those two could delay the anticipation of an inevitable. There was no question they were meant for each other. What could go wrong with a gorgeous forty-nine years old man going on thirty-nine? This was the only lie that existed in their new life. In his defense, he did not look older than thirty-six, even when he was tired or sick.

His apartment was on the top floor overlooking the ocean. The bedroom balcony window was open, and fresh air penetrated thin curtains. She was standing by the opposite side of the bed and looking at him, taking off his sport coat. In a deemed nightstand light, she could see every muscle on his chest under a thin white t-shirt. No one was making a sound. He stared at her standing six feet away from him. She was silently praying to all powers of her universe. She wanted him. She wanted him to be as fantastic in bed as he was outside of it. And as anything she ever wished for with an open heart, it happened.

A second and six fit closer. He was slowly demanding, hovering her mouth. His strong fingers were sliding down her back, carefully unzipping her dress. She was fully naked, sitting on the side of the bed in front of him. She waited to see him taking his clothes off. Instead, he knelt and proposed to her everything she had prayed for a minute earlier. How long do ordinary people in love have sex? Usually, it takes a little over an hour to talk about grown adults. He did not let go of her for over three and a half hours, not stopping for anything, no water, no bathroom break, no phone check. And no, those two did not smoke, they did not drink alcohol, and they did not do any drugs. They were pure, and what was happening that night in that airy bedroom was pure magic.

CHAPTER 5

Right Timing

"It was always the right time to her"

Right timing. Putting your life on hold. An excuse to take your responsibilities into your hands. She had fifty years of life experience in her thirties. Seven different lives in different places with various people. It was always the right time for everything. She did not like to wait to live and to feel. Nothing scared her. Her second husband almost died in a car accident, driving to meet her on their first date. An average person would think ten times about pursuing a relationship starting like that. But it was not her. She did not believe in the right timing. It was always the right time for her.

There is a tendency in Seeking Arrangement's male profiles. Everyone above fifty years old would write down that they are forty-nine. And if they were above sixty, they would be fifty-nine; hundreds of forty-nine- and fifty-nine-years older men in her city alone. Getting a message from a fifty-one-year-old was another whole game. His profile had no photo with a minimal description of the person he was comfortable enough to reveal about himself. Her favorite usual: intelligent, athletic, bilingual, great sense of humor, wealthy with a love for food and travel. With children "Prefer Not To Say" answer and married. Discretion above all. Basic, if not to say much. He could be anyone, but she did not want anyone. She wanted someone unusual and very special.

For six months, they would plan to meet and never meet. For six months, she deleted his contact and saved it again. There was no actual texting. No one asked questions. No one shared any personal information or preferences. At some point, he revealed a picture of himself. He was handsome and her type. If it were anyone else, those men would be blocked from canceling or rescheduling a date with her, but this guy was wasting her time the way it did not feel like it was wasted. She let him pick any day, place, or time, knowing he would cancel all of it days before. Time was approaching, and it was a day before exactly six months like he wrote her on Seeking. A long text message came in from him. This time he was not canceling. He was confirming and instructing her how to get to him discretely. "Discretion is a must" was mentioned multiple times.

Finding a high-end luxury hotel with unrestricted use of elevators is rare. For those who travel a lot, we know you get a card or a fab for an elevator. Otherwise, there is no way you are getting to your place of staying. Guests must go to the hotel's front desk and notify them where they are going, and they activate the elevator for you. Strangely this hotel was an exception. And she did not know about it. How could she? He did not say anything about elevators either.

The number of angry text messages she got in those two minutes of the distance between his front desk and his suite was something out of a funny American comedy. He opened the door and let her into his living room. Freshly showered, he was wrapped head to toe into a huge white robe, fluffy white hotel flippers covered his toes. She did not even have time to say "Hi."

He screamed and ran around like a crazy person.

"How could you do this to them? Why did you go to the front desk? Bad, bad, bad. Now, everyone knows a beautiful woman is in my room. Everyone knows! And everyone knows me! Why did you do it to me? You have to leave right away."

She was standing in her girly crotched white day dress in the sunlight coming into the room thru curtains. Her natural blond hair was sparking like a ray of sunshine. She was silently smiling and looking at him without understanding what was happening. She could sense all the good and kindness in him, hidden in an avatar of this cute, gone-mad Bugs Bunny in a fluffy white robe. She liked him instantly. The situation was hilarious. He stopped screaming for a second, and she explained the elevator confusion. She could not believe he was asking her to leave immediately.

Who does that?

Well, exactly six months of the wrong timing.

Driving home, she could not stop thinking something very important did not happen. It was obvious. He was far from being basic or usual. He was clinically retarded if he chose to let her go.

CHAPTER 6

Second Chances

"People are most honest and truthful when they just wake up"

Second chances. Who deserves second chances? Even the most self-aware women with healthy consciousness once or twice a month have difficulty controlling themselves during days around their period. Hormones are little devils. Men don't have this problem. There should be no real reason to forgive men for their fits.

It has been eight days and eight nights since she dealt with rejection. No, she was not lonely, and she was busy. Her workplace needed her full-time this week, but during breaks in her training sessions, her mind would take her back to that day. A man in a white robe would cross her mind on a drive to and from work. And every evening dining out with her friends, she would scan the room to look for mad Bugs Bunny. After all, he was a foodie, and they were in the same habitat.

She woke up before her alarm that morning. It was rare. The number of things she did in one day would make her sleep like a dead person from the moment her head touched her pillow till the usual seven fifteen am she had to wake up. His name showed on the lock screen of her iPhone. She was sleepy, and she read every word twice not to miss any hidden meaning in between words.

He was generous with words. "Good morning, I had a dream last night, and you were present. I have decided to write you to tell you how sorry I feel about the situation that happened the other day. I hope you can accept my apology, but discretion is a must for me, and this hotel is (here he gave up the information about who he is, and this should stay discrete because he took a chance to trust her). I wish you all the best in your life."

His message came in at 05.21 a.m. People are most honest and truthful when they wake up. It was romantic. And she responded.

They have texted every day for hours for two months. They knew everything about each other and nothing about their personal life. Since the day he apologized, she gave him a chance to love each other, and there was a lot to love about them. He was reading a book she recommended on his 21-hour flight to Asia while she watched his favorite movie on her way to Buenos Aires. She complained that she kept changing the décor in her bedroom because she did not feel at home there, and he was complementing her good taste in classical art. He figured out how to build the life of his dreams when he was seventeen, while she just started to love herself at thirty. He openly shared his lack of patience life stories, and she copied/pasted explanations of self-regulation of mental processes from her psychological studies to him. She amused him, and he inspired her. They had fights, and he was always the one to smooth it out. Every day. They texted and texted, and they had never run out of things to tell each other until he told her he wanted nothing more than to kiss her.

Lunch was delicious, and she was so excited she could not eat. She wanted to go up to the room, and she wanted to be able to touch him without worrying about someone seeing them. But he kept ordering desert after desert and playing on her nerves. She never liked sweets anyway.

On the way up, they discussed his unpleasant business meeting last night, but all she could think was how his freshly shaved face would feel on her skin. She leaned towards his lips as soon as his suite door was locked. It was a perfect fit. He was a perfect height, and her arms rested on his shoulders, playing with the back of his head. His full puffy lips were heaven for her mouth. He kissed the same way she kissed. Two intelligent, mature adults kissed like teenagers for almost three hours straight. They made up a kingdom where he was a king, and she would be punished with tickles if she tried to talk. Out of this horrifying fear, she did not talk at all.

Sometimes when you master the art of meditation, you can zone out to a sensory world without time or thoughts. A magical energy exchange had to happen for two people to experience the same sensation simultaneously for long hours while kissing. They had the same heartbeat, and at that moment, they forgot who they were and how important their lives were to others, and they let go of their responsibilities for other people and dissolved in each other.

He wanted her all. She felt it thru his clothes. He would pleasure her body inch by inch, not letting her touch his. She had to wait until their second date to have one of the most amazing lovemaking of her life. It is amazing how someone as busy as him would not be in a rush at all with her.

Every time they deliberately crossed paths at long layovers between their independent travel, she would look at him coming out through the international customs door and remembering him screaming and running around like a crazy person in a white robe the day they met. And he would always look at her smile and know exactly what she was thinking.

CHAPTER 7

Loving with Blindfold on

*"Our childhood is a box with instructions
and operation manuals to our mind".*

O ur childhood is a box with instructions and operation
manuals in our minds. If you willingly dig out that box
and start reading where all your ideas, worries, and preferences
started, you might finally understand yourself and push a reset
button if you want to start over. The problem is old buttons
tend to get stuck. It would look like a grown man found a way
to go back in time and start his life over at age seven while
keeping all his life knowledge with him. As a result, he would
be a smart kid with an ambition to rule the world while having
no power to do so because at seven years old, all you can do
is play video games, and you are afraid to leave your house
without your parents.

His Seeking profile was always the first thing she saw logging in online—great professionally taken photo. The profile was filled up with information about its owner. He was exceptional, extraordinary. He was not hiding anything and was clear on who he was inviting into his life. He was the person everyone would love to get a piece of, but as a man, he was not of interest to her.

She did not remember why she wrote him, it might have been a lonely evening, or she took it as a sign his profile was always in front of everything else she was diving into that any other day. He said she seemed remarkable, but it did not seem like they were looking for the same thing. And he was right. She already knew that.

Year passed. Everything changed, and nothing changed. She was looking for the next arrangement to feel, love, and get inspired before the subject of her desires tried to tie her up in a traditional relationship she avoided. It was not because she was against it. It was because she loved herself more, and her enjoyment of her freedom outweighed any scenarios offered to her. She was unapologetically self-sufficient mentally, emotionally, physically, and financially. Change in her relationship status from "*single*" to "*taken*" was only up to her desire to do so, and at the moment, there was no need to change anything in this department of her life.

The same profile rejecting her undefined interest in the past was trying to get her attention. He wanted to meet her. He left his full name and asked to Google him and to contact him on his cell phone number. It was unnecessary. She did not Google people and trusted her inner feelings, wisdom and analytical mind to evaluate possible future partners. If you Googled her, you would find a description of her as she was yesterday or pursuing a past carrier or relationship. Nothing you could Google to find out who she was today and what was going on in her life because the real her was unavailable to anyone outside of her small circle.

She responded to him with an offer of a friendly dinner since what he wanted from her as a woman, and she was simply unable to provide. They set a dinner time five days in advance. The next day he called her, and surprisingly they spoke on the phone for two and a half hours.

There is so much love, kindness, and positivity in her, and everyone loves her. Her opinions were fresh and innovative. Her smart, sarcastic humor could penetrate anyone's cold heart or closed mind. And just like that, most interesting people on Earth could not stop thinking about her.

He had his face on all major political magazine covers, he was a brilliant specialist in his chosen profession, and he was a personal friend to a list of presidents of countries at war. Winning battles was his favorite thing. He was getting medals to keep, while others ruled their countries by his scenario. Millions of people's lives depended on his chosen cause of action. And this guy could not find himself a place in his own house waiting for her to join him for dinner.

She had never seen anything like that. The level of security and the number of cameras in and out of his penthouse was something out of Jason Borne's movies. A fortress in the sky, surrounded by normal relaxed residents of this dream-like megapolis. He never left his penthouse, and everyone had to come to him to pick his mind or get his money. He smiled when she signed his non-disclosure agreement. He had a beautiful, welcoming smile of a child, genuine and inviting. She suddenly desired to hug him but was unsure it was allowed in his game.

He wanted to control all of her. And she would gladly let him if he only possessed one quality. He needed to have a heart bigger than hers. She knew he did not, but she hoped to swell his heart and enlarge it by giving him hers. She put a blindfold on and followed him into the darkest of darks.

CHAPTER 8

Those Who Don't Believe in Magic

"They did not seem to agree on things,
be he could not stop talking to her".

Things we do to ourselves. Even the best of us once in a while tend to cross to the other side and live by the desires of our mind, while all our life, we are building the infrastructure to live by our heart's desires only. Unconsciously, we always know when something is not right. Only the bravest of us react instantly.

She was holding her third cup of hot green tea in her hands. He was sitting at his work desk in his home office. It was dark, and the room was filled with cigarette smoke. He was not smoking, he would light them up individually and let them burn on their own in his hand. Four hours long conversation on all non-related topics about the balance of our existence.

He wanted to free nations from tyrants. But he did not believe in murdering them. She believed death is the most productive and fast solution to rapid change. They did not seem to agree, but he could not stop talking to her.

She was half-naked in a big office chair before him. She liked him. She desired him physically and romantically. If she was lucky and the moment was right, he would kiss her in a month or put his hand around her back. Rarely, once or twice. It was enough to give her a glimpse of hope to bring out the man she desired. She found his foot under a table and rubbed it with her toe. He moved further away from her.

An hour watching him test a newly developing video game. Always a battle-winner with the highest scores. He would play every night for an hour, never longer. Her son played the same games back at her apartment exactly at this hour. Millions of people did play these same games. If they only knew who they were playing with or against. Having him as a player on your side could skyrocket your productivity instantly. Real-life world leaders knew that. And he knew he was the best of his kind and irreplaceable for people of power.

Spending hours in his bedroom, she was coming out hungry for a gentle touch, a cuddle, a kiss. It was frustrating. He was brilliant at making love with zero emotions. If you can put a strategy in capturing a woman's body, his battle plan of action would win this contest.

Cigarette smoke was burning her eyes. He was talking about regressions into past lives and making fun of an exceptional psychiatrist whose life work helped her to find her inner peace a few years back. And then she realized something. He could not see a major point in his colleague's discovery. He was missing the key to the door, which could take his understanding of the soul's evolution to the end, where everything was simple and clear. He could not feel love. He wanted to, but it was not possible in the mindset he was living in. Emotionally they were two opposites.

She hated dark places, and she hated any smoke. She hated control and being told what she couldn't do. If she got up right this second and hugged him – he would push her away from him. Cruel gentle monster. She was killing herself, trying to save him. It had to stop.

He finished his video game and expressed his desire to turn their arrangement into a full-time relationship. Her nightmare in an evening light. To this day, she did not understand how he could believe it was possible. She got up and exited his office without asking his permission. He was telling her something, it was something about him being very nice to her, and he did not understand what was going on. She truly wanted to explain to him he should have never met her because those who don't believe in magic will never have it.

CHAPTER 9

Puzzled Danger

"The rule of living dangerously stands on the ability to read in between the lines and knowing when enough is enough"

D anger. A regular human being knows only the idea of the feeling of danger. It is a feeling inside their head—the feeling of the unknown. The real danger is only a friend to those not afraid to live. Some prefer to be married to danger, some to date it occasionally. It is like a drug, a constant adrenalin rush. It is exciting. Exciting until the moment you get physically hurt.

The rule of living dangerously stands on the ability to read between the lines and know when enough is enough.

She grew up in a third-world country surrounded by wonderful children with no opportunities available to them after high school. Girls had it better. They suffered freely. Boys not knowing how and where to go turned into imprisoned alcoholics, drug addicts, and criminals. At fourteen, she was in love with an older boy, he was nineteen, and he was kind and funny. He always made sure she was safe and happy. She cried for months when he was arrested for a warehouse robbery.

At seventeen, her lover was married thirty-one-year-old lawyer. He was very good at legally stealing housing from people experiencing poverty and growing his real estate portfolio. Every Sunday, she would join him for brunch with the local judge and police captain. He taught her a great quality to find a way to enjoy everything she was doing. A few months after she moved to a bigger city to study at the university, his friend, a police captain, drove three hundred kilometers just to tell her in person her lover was shot, and it was not clear if he would recover. It did not matter to her; he was her past.

At her twenty, very energetic fifty-two years old, never married no kids' gentlemen started to shower her with top designer gifts and the best spa and restaurant experiences available in the country they were living in. On a first date, he told her his name was not his real name. On the second date, he introduced her to his parents, which was the first time he brought a girl home. She noticed they were constantly being followed and watched on a third date. He was overprotective and thoughtful. He thought about every single detail. He wanted to be with her every available to him second, and he chose her to build a family with. Eating out with his closest friends was an event with funny stories about conspiracies and murders during the nineties in post-Soviet Union times. Four months in, she was asked not to leave their apartment without the driver. She liked it. All this possible danger and his great care for her were exciting. Until one day, she was walking down to the car by herself. She walked two flights of stairs when he started screaming from above for her to stop walking further down immediately. She has never heard his voice so loud and panicky. Walking back up, she heard fireworks going out outside. Fireworks in the late Tuesday morning, too close and too loud. It was odd. A few hours later, she saw one of his cars penetrated by thousand bullets standing right in front of the entrance to their apartment building. After that event, she decided never in her life to put herself in danger ever again. Meeting people online can put inexperienced people into paranoia. Women can be hurt, raped, or killed. Men can be drugged, robbed, or blackmailed. And not many can be harassed by the Federal Bureau of Investigation or watched by Central Intelligence Agency.

His profile was open and friendly. The late forties, a very well-educated doctor turned businessman, grown children, divorced, in an great physical shape with similar interests as her. He joined Seeking yesterday, and it was the only thing she did not like about his profile. People new to the concept of an arranged relationship rarely knew what they were looking for, so it always turned into drama and major time-wasting for the women they sought to meet. And, of course, he wanted to meet her.

In such situations, she would be straightforward and throw all her wishes and demands at a newbie in her first response. He has replied "yes" to everything. He wanted to meet her immediately. She called him to make sure he was a real person. He was communicating in a way like they knew each other for years. He was practically finishing up her sentences. He was so easy and pleasant; it felt like he had known her for years. Something very strange but innocent was about him. He was too easy and too agreeable for an intelligent person.

She was always great at puzzles. She thought her very last control freak arranged boyfriend was playing a joke on her. She invited her new agreeable friend for tea to her apartment the next day, being sure her hurt and abounded ex-lover would show up instead.

Finding parking or entering the self-sufficient modern building she lived in was difficult. Without any instructions, a tall, handsome man entered her living room. He spoke about his life, his children and his work, his volunteering at the military bases in the Middle East, and his constant international travel. He made sure he had no intentions of pursuing any physical contact with her today. It was the second mistake he made. If she was not the reason he came in today, then what was?

After his third mistake of knowing what color and made her car was, she put down her cup of hot green tea and asked him if he had come in on official business. He smiled. He said that she seemed like a great person and a great mom. He said that he does not like some of her friends. He said some of her friends are dangerous bad men. He got up and started to walk out of her apartment. At the door, he turned around and said it was great meeting her.

She never sold that puzzle. The reason she was on the spot could have been a few people in her today's life. And all of them were very nice to her.

CHAPTER 10

Everything She Ever Wanted

"Ten days post legal completion of his divorce,
he finally decided to live his life for himself and it is a huge
decision to make for any good family man"

For the last twenty years, she must have met over thousand men. Everyday life, work, online, traveling, and all other possible ways. Being pretty; and sweet to everyone was like an invitation for men to approach her, even if she did not intend to be approached. Online was her preferred way of meeting people. Thirty to seventy men daily would contact her to get a time of her day or night.

Online requires the least amount of time, and it is more productive than meeting people at bars or in an aisle of a grocery store. Online profiles give you an overall idea of who the person is and what they want. The Seeking Arrangement platform did much more. It let you be honest about your differences and preferences, needs, and wants. There was no judgment, and it was supposed to be no drama. Until one of the two in an arranged relationship fell in love, imagine the amount of drama if both partners fell in.

It was a time of her life when she was absolutely happy with everyone and everything in it. The sadness from the separation from her second husband has faded, and she was convinced love will find her again. Or she will find love herself.

His profile description started with the words "I am going to be absolutely honest". And he was honest about his age and a few other things. At first sight, he was a guy next door, friendly and funny, easy-going and kind. He loved people and himself. Twenty years of marriage and a couple of grown kids on his resume. Self-made and at a time in his life with zero worries in it.

On their first date, he told her he wanted to have as much fun and as many women as possible. Ten days after post legal completion of his divorce, he finally decided to live his life for himself, which is a huge decision for any good family man. He did not want to feel deep or get attached; he wanted uncondi-tional sexualized fun. She laughed and said: "I will leave you as soon as you fall in love with me, and everyone does."

He loved sex as much as she did. They fucked for hours before lunch and for hours after. Hungry, they would walk hand in hand to nearby restaurants and joke with everyone about everything at lunch. She would take a day off work a week and spend it with him. Those other six days in between some weeks felt like an eternity. Other weeks would fly by like few hours. She would look at the screen on her iPhone more and more, hoping to see his text. He was wonderful about respecting their separate lives while not on a "together" day. He never texted anything except to confirm their meeting next week. It was right, and for some reason, it bothered her.

Somehow "together" day got longer, he would take her to all new restaurants in town for dinners, and they would play food critics like children. They went to movies, art galleries, and parks. They did grocery shopping, and he always ensured he bought her thoughtful gifts from all her favorite stores. He sent beautiful flowers to her apartment. They danced and read books together. They took baths and naps. One day he mentioned he would like to meet a nice woman his age and start to date again. Women with no children or grown children can travel and live their life on the fly. She knew it could not possibly be her. She was a single mother to a young boy, working full-time, and her travel dates were tied to a county's school schedule. But she liked him, and deep inside, she wanted to be that woman. So, she found a woman his age for him.

She introduced them at a local event. She was impatiently waiting to see if her matchmaking skills were a success. That was when she did not know he did not need any help meeting women. When she heard from a possible match that a woman did not like her secret lover, she felt she could breathe again. And it all became clear. She realized she wanted him for herself only, full-time and in the real world.

Summer vacations were approaching, and she flew off with her son to discover another side of the planet. He went on vacation with his kids and friends. Not having "together" days for weeks lifted the restriction on keeping contact. They texted like teenagers every day, all day, and all night. All her messages were responded to instantly. Something wonderful was happening to them both. She wondered if he noticed that too.

They could not get their hands off each other the next time they met. He told her he missed her dearly, and she suggested they start dating like normal people. And then, unexpectedly, he reminded her how she laughed at him the first time they met. Making fun of her accent, he quoted: "I will leave you as soon as you fall in love with me, and everyone does," and he drove off into the night.

She entered her building and walked up to her apartment, her son was telling her something, but she could not hear. She could not focus at all. It was a dark, cold blur. Twenty minutes after, he called her and told her he would be stupid not to date her.

CHAPTER 11

People Who Want to Change

"There are fantastic people walking among us who choose not to feel, because feeling of "not feeling" they can control"

People change. Incorrect. Only people who want to change – change. The feeling of being in love with someone you barely know blinds you. Suddenly a smart and mature adult becomes happy running around nerve wrack. And under that pressure, everything inside us, invisible to the human eye, emerges. All problems and misunderstandings from previous relationships are projected onto this new innocent person who loves you.

It was the happiest few months of her life. Nothing she ever felt came close to this. She felt complete. They were inseparable. They were happy. Happy anywhere doing anything or not doing anything at all. He knew what she was going to say.

before she said it. He had the same fierce outlook on life as her. She loved him, she loved absolutely everything about him, and she loved herself loving him. The vision of her future changed completely. She no longer needed to conquer anything or anyone in the world. He had everything she needed and wanted from life. She deleted her Seeking profile and took her guard down, and she let him in, and he came in with all his mental issues and insecurities, which destroyed her and their perfectly happy relationship.

It never occurred to her fifty-two years old man had never loved before, he had never experienced the feeling of romantic jealousy, and he was not able to trust anyone at all. He would not talk to her for days if she did not respond to his text within the next fifteen minutes. He called her every few hours to not lose track of her. He would sit her down every day and tell her she was doing something wrong. Some days he made her cry. She might be the happiest person you will ever meet. She never cried. The happier she was – the less he smiled.

It took her months to see what was happening. He loved her so much, but he was not emotionally prepared to handle it. Emotionally he had as much experience as a fifteen years old boy. His love was hurting him, not knowing how to live with it. He wanted to be happy with her, but he could not. Like a blind can't see or a deaf can't hear. He could not let himself be happy. And this is real. Fantastic people are walking among us who choose not to feel because the feeling of "not feeling" they can control. And no one could control her.

But this was not the actual problem they had. She never paid attention to his weekly meetings with his psychologist. She liked the fact he felt comfortable getting mental health. The odd thing was he was seeing a psychologist all his life. Even with her little background in psychology, she knew someone who would undergo help like that all their life was not cable of regulating their mental processes by themselves. His inability to do so left him constantly anxious and worrying about everything. And that is when the desire to control everything and everyone came in.

Fighting for love got a whole new meaning for her. There were no other people between them, no unfinished businesses with exes, no desire to explore relationships with other people. She was fighting an invisible enemy inside his head.

And one weekday evening, having dinner with him at another new restaurant in town, she could not remember when she saw him smiling last time. Here he was: handsome, healthy, smart, successful, funny, kind, caring wonderful person, a father, a brother, a son, a friend, and to add to all that fortune, he had her. He had her. And still, he was not happy. She got up and left.

People say to forget someone or something you need time or new emotions. New people. New places. New situations. She gave herself the full green light for all that new. It was the most reckless time of her life, and it did not work. Numerous men and women brought great new into her life, but no one could love her as he did.

People say you need to give yourself time to heal. She let him go, and she loved other men after him. She let go of the hope of reconnecting with him, but she never healed. She couldn't. How can two free souls love each other so deeply and not be able to be together?

CHAPTER 12

Coming Back Home

*"Last thing she wanted is to make anyone feel uncomfortable
by who she was and how she lived her life and
what she spent her money on"*

New life. New online profile. New pictures. New wishes and new desires. Coming back to Seeking Arrangement was like coming back home. It had everything she liked in one place. She could not wait to get on the highest rollercoaster and get feeling. She never smoked, drank alcohol, or did drugs. Everything she ever felt was pure and real. Some days she was high on life. On other days she was high on herself. And all day, everyone else was high on her.

New profiles on Seeking did not have a history of previous messages between members. If you do not have a good memory of faces or profile details, you could go on a first date with someone you have been on a date with once before. You could go on a date with someone who already got pissed off by you and left you in the middle of the dinner by yourself.

Her memory was impeccable. What was not impeccable is the intentions of men who wish to have what they can't afford, so they lie and make you a part of their scam. Time wasters. She was looking at his profile, wondering why they had not met in the past. He was a member for the last seven years, and she believed she knew all men in this city with Seeking history length like that. That was the part in your profile you could not edit yourself. It screamed of experience in this type of relationship. He was a very good-looking, stylish former family man with decent business, athletic, well-traveled, and all other good characteristics she preferred in men.

In his proposal to her, he was beyond generous in his offerings. He could be a long run for a very long run. Fitting him into her lunch break time, he was instructed to show up at her most convenient lunch spot. Thanks to her second husband, she loved food, and the places she chose to eat at now were the best in town.

She spotted him waiting for her sitting at her favorite table. Good sign, she thought. They had a great conversation accompanied by her favorite sushi. What were the odds they were in Barcelona at the same time last summer and stayed in hotels on the same square? He was pleasant and funny. Almost too nice for her taste. Almost too nice to be true.

They had so much fun she canceled the rest of her appointments for the afternoon. There was one more thing to check if he was as great in bed as he was at talking. That would be Beginner's Luck on a second try! After getting a check, they walked to their cars, and he told her a story about his sisters. He was telling her a story she knew already. This was not their first date, but is she the only one who has realized it?

Years before today, at the very beginning of her Seeking Arrangement journey, she did not know what she was seeking in this 'new to her' arranged type of relationship. It is when, once before, she met this guy. They had dinner at this same

39

restaurant, and he was twenty minutes late. They sat at this same, her favorite, table, and she ordered the same food.

He was arrogant and jumpy. She would answer every question he asked. She was excited and happy they had met. He would tell her stories about his daughter and his sisters. She loved listening to him, he was surrounded by his wonderful women and all that care what came with it. Men with families like that are loving, caring, and gentle. He looked excited too. In a bit strange way, but excited! She took it as his nerves were upon him. She used to get nervous on a first date too, especially if she liked someone more than usual.

He complimented her on her Van Cleef jewelry and her gold Rolex Daytona watch by naming the brands and models exactly what they are. It felt odd. If any men ever complimented her on her things, they would say things like "Your earrings are beautiful" or "I have this same watch" or something like that.

She doubted some of them even knew how much all that was worth. This guy knew, and by the tone of his voice, he had a problem with her wearing that. And then he asked the strangest question ever: "So you don't need anything from me?".

Maybe she wanted it to be a question, but in reality, it probably was not a question. It was a statement. What an odd thing to ask. She wanted to know how his lips would feel on her neck and if he was making love or fucking type, but she could not say it out loud. So, she responded: "No, I don't need anything from you", and she gave him a big beautiful genuine smile.

He got up so fast his chair fell back on the floor. He threw a fifty-dollar bill on the table and left.

She was never bothered by other people around her, and everyone was always watching her no matter what she did, where she was, or who she was with. She lighted up any room she was in. She finished her food and got the bill. His fifty-dollar bill did not even cover his drinks.

Later on, in her mind, she would go back to that dinner repeatedly until she realized she was too expensive for him. And that is fine. The last thing she wanted was to make anyone uncomfortable with who she was, how she lived her life, and what she spent her money on.

And now, years after, they reconnected again. She was driving, and he followed her in his car into her parking garage. She touched her ears and realized she was wearing those same Van Cleef earrings and the same Rolex Daytona watch today, in addition to other diamonds. But him, he is so different this time. How strange. They parked their cars, and she came close to him. He looked so genuinely happy. Perhaps she shouldn't bring the past back, but if they hit it off and started seeing each other, she would have to keep this to herself indefinitely. She hated lying or being lied to. So, she told him what she remembered and watched his reaction. He looked surprised, and he laughed. He said: "No way it was you. That girl was so unpleasant". And without thinking over his feedback or his actions on their first date, she wrapped her body around his, and thirty minutes later, they were lying all sweaty and happy on her bed sheets.

He was talking about all that they would do next together. It was nice. She was fully satisfied emotionally and physically. He got dressed, and he left. He never texted or called her again. That was the last time they saw each other.

CHAPTER 13

Proper Life

"Proper life. Society standards inflicted upon us at childhood by our imperfect parents trying to make up for their mistakes at our cost"

Proper life. Society's standards are inflicted upon us in childhood by our imperfect parents trying to make up for their mistakes at our cost. Simple expectations of graduating with the highest grades, getting a driver's license as soon as possible, doing well in sports or a chess club, finishing university, becoming a doctor or a lawyer or an accountant, marrying a nice girl/boy next door and pass on this proper circle of life to your children. Some extra icing on the cake is to stay married to the same person all your life and live your life not to disappoint your neighbors. And she did just that first thirty years of her life. He did the same for fifty-six until he met her.

His Seeking profile was proper, and it was responsibly filled out. The handsome doctor sought a muse to explore

everything missing in his marriage. She did not like the part
he was local, but being married should keep him in check not
to try to bother her too much and too often. Usually, anyone
not agreeing right away on the arrangement terms she wanted
would be moved to the "not qualified" folder. He insisted on
meeting in person and discussing her terms in person because
it was important to him. It sounded odd not to say much, but
she was in a great mood and had lots of energy that day, so
she agreed on a meeting of uncertainty, a potential one to two
hours of lost time in her day. Some people fed homeless kit-
tens, others pored soup at homeless shelters, and she gifted her
priceless energy and free time to strangers when she felt like
doing so.

Busy high-end touristic hotel's lobby had a coffee shop.
She and coffee had a special relationship. She did not need coffee, but when she was in the hand proximity of a coffee shop,
it was a special treat. Coffee made her speak even faster, and
her eyes sparkled even brighter. It was the wrong thing to do
before meeting someone who didn't know her yet, but having
a cup of almond milk latte felt better than this idea of possible
wasted time.

She was paying for her order when she spotted him at the
entrance to the coffee shop. He was a typical American-looking
working man with a dad body. He could not possibly be local
in this city. He did not fit it. She smiled wide and did a sharp
turn towards him. Her dress flew up in the air and did a full
circle around her hips. She looked spectacular in the daylight
coming in from the glass ceiling.

A married man chooses one of the busiest places in town
to meet a beautiful young woman. It screamed either of inex-
perience in an infidelity matter or of simple stupidity. And
right after they officially greeted each other, he asked her if
she wanted to meet his brother in the lobby. Thank God she
got that coffee. This meeting was getting more and more

ridiculous. The whole point of an arranged relationship is to skip regular nonsense like meeting arranged partner's friends or co-workers or whatever else normal people have to do not to upset their partners.

Thankfully she has learned how to say a firm "no" and stand her ground in the last few years of being single, so she took him to the pool garden, and they sat in a shaded cabana while she was enjoying her coffee. He was inexperienced. He was honest, and he was nice about everything. He was a talented and respectable member of a global importance society. That explained his appearance and posture. Have you ever seen casual photos of Warren Buffet and Bill Gates together? This guy's look could join theirs like Bill Gates' twin.

By the time he finished his brief life story, caffeine had taken full control of her senses, she had opened her mouth to say one word, and she accidentally told him a short version of all her mid-thirties biography. Her mimic was on a level of an experienced comedian. She laughed, her eyes rolled, and if someone recorded all her jokes and sarcastic statements, that book would delight you before you started reading this one.

An hour passed. She was convinced she scared this nice traditional man to the point he would go back to his online profile right this second and delete it, not to deal with weird women like her ever again. Instead, he was fascinated by her. He agreed to all her arrangement demands, he thanked her for meeting him, and they planned to meet again next week.

That evening he came home to his wife and kids. He had a simple meal cooked by his house cook, he went to his office and deleted his Seeking profile. He found what he was looking for.

CHAPTER 14

Illusions

*"Illusions we create in our lives help us survive
the reality we chose for ourselves rarely make
us happy at the end of the day"*

Illusions we create in our lives help us survive the reality we chose for ourselves and rarely make us happy at the end of the day. When his starter pack studies were completed and time and age came to terms to move on to the next proper life stage, like starting a family and having kids, he made a list of qualities a proper wife and a mother of his offspring should have, and he married the one qualified. Twenty years after, he was looking back at his lifeless house and his family, where love never visited, where kids never saw their parents touch hands, where he was never appreciated for his life achievements and for providing a comfortable, relaxed life to his "loved ones."

Illusions we create when we meet a new person blind us hard with a feeling of being in love. Deep inside, he saw himself in that energetic, happy young woman and lost any sense of reality.

He started to push the limits of her non-negotiable arrangement after their romantic first date. He wanted to change the terms. Despite him being extremely busy and her not ever offering her own extra time to him, he needed to see her more often. That first romantic afternoon they spent together was wonderful. Nothing needed to say except "Thank you" on both sides, but she was walking out of the hotel room running away from him and his words: "How wonderful it would be if we did it every day".

She really liked him. He was smart, considerate, always responsible, and not having much practice in marital affairs, most importantly, he was fantastic in bed. They laughed, and the hours they spent together weekly were priceless until he would start to lose his reality and express his desire to be together and have more children with her. She hoped this was some certain "blah-blah want to be" game for him until he would bring up his suggestions on "their" future life every time they met.

They were walking the streets of Charleston holding hands, he tried to please her in ways he thought she would be pleased, but he never got to see who she was. All he needed to do was listen to what she was saying as it was. Instead, he would mentally place himself in her future plans while drifting away from her reality. He was pushing his perfect imaginable future on her, and she started to feel uncomfortable. He was turning their wonderful simple arrangement into a delusional daytime nightmare.

She silently walked to dinner. He was happy they would not speak and still be so comfortable together in silence. At dinner, he told her how they would travel to wonderful places and how much he wanted to have a daughter with her. She did not remember if she smiled today at all. She lifted her eyes from her pasta and asked him: "Do you remember you are married?".

The next morning, she woke up and started to pack her luggage, wanting to make it to the airport early and hundred percent make it home and back to her happy single simple real world today. He was watching her from behind his phone, and he said: "I can't wait for us to wake up like this together every morning".

There was a fantastic family-owned little café at the airport, and she enjoyed southern food and her almond milk latte. She was smiling, and she was happy to go back home. He was sitting across the small table from her. He was telling her about his relationship with his children. She was listening, and she did not know how to tell him that he did not have a relationship with his children. His non-existing relationship with his wife pushed him so far away from his children that she doubted he could ever cross that ocean. And he wanted to have another child with her. How could a bright, successful good man fuck up his family life so badly? There was nothing she could do to help him, and she was silently waiting for their flight to start boarding. He was draining the life out of her. And then, when you think nothing could go even more unpleasant, he suggested they would marry.

She was the type of person who would never raise her voice or scream or yell at anyone. She avoided conflicts with people by simply talking openly about the arising issues. But that day, a beautiful young woman was screaming at an older gentleman she was traveling with, involving the whole wing in an airport into their conflict. Now, everyone knew this gentleman forgot he was a married man. He was mentally abusing this beautiful young woman with his delusional ideas of their possible happy family, which he never got to have in the first place.

On the return flight home, she was going back in time to try to understand when she ever gave him the idea he had a chance to be a part of her real life outside of their arrangement relationship. She was always herself. She was smiling and laughing, and she was happy and satisfied, but never once she said anything to make him believe she had a desire to see him for more than a few hours a week. Never.

As soon as the cockpit door was open, she walked out of the plane and made sure she never saw him again.

CHAPTER 15

The Unrules

"Even if it is a scam, she felt this will be a fun one to live thru"

Men of Seeking Arrangement are constantly harassed by scammers, drug-and-rob, and blackmailed by estranged SA's website women. Good guys are being taken advantage of for their generosity to strangers in trouble. Some being stood up on their dates. Some are purely used as ATM machines. There is as much trash online as in real life, you have to keep a positive attitude and dig through the garbage. Similar unfortunate events happen to women of Seeking Arrangement as well. You must work hard and be positive to meet someone with a "wow" factor. Or you get an assistant. Take aggressive risks, but manage losses.

All theories and all methods have flaws. His profile was sample-like. Nothing gave any insights into who he was as a person. Profile of a successful fifty years old educated, married man with children, income over million dollars a year, and net worth over a hundred million. There was nothing personal except for the part where it was stated "He needs an elegant, understanding lady with a flexible schedule, very pleasant and sweet over text." When she got to the word "text," she realized it was a scam. A man on the other line wants to waste her time and get off on it. She did not respond to his message asking for her name and offer to text on WhatsApp about a possible arrangement.

Events don't unfold as anticipated, so there are limits to what can be planned. Persistence compounds your ability. The next day same profile messaged her again. He saw she checked out his profile and read his previous message. What happened next was new to her on her Seeking journey. Something new in a few years. Another woman introduced herself by name and stated her position as a personal assistant to a man described in this profile. She explained how busy her employer was and what arrangements she tried to help him find. She gave a few more details about a man with this mysterious profile. She explained what unpleasant situations he has been through with women on this site, and that is where she came in to get him through an initial casting process to a final "audition" in person.

Knowledge grows from knowledge, and good ideas constitute new knowledge, altering reality in growth.

She read this long, very explanatory message written by a woman trusted to pick a perfect mistress for her employer, and she wanted to believe this was all real. The part where this man's description as a person who checked all her desired boxes did not help her think. Her brain was in love already. Even if it was a scam, she felt this would be a fun one to live through. She decided to join their game. Thinking big is always easier. She picked up her iPhone and texted her real name to a personal number of a mystery man.

He wanted her to meet him in Vancouver, and she said the first meeting would be in her town, and it was non-negotiable. He sent her selfies almost every day of his deadly serious face from cities in different countries, and she was jokingly responding about how much she liked his smile. Fifteen days of texting, joking, and laughing. She landed back home from another vacation trip with her son and texted her new mystery admirer a photo of a beautiful tropical sunset she just took when they were landing. He responded with a screenshot from his phone with a photo album with over eight thousand sunset pictures taken through the window of his plane. Explain that. Quantity is quality.

She woke up to his message asking what she would like to do on the evening of the first day of the next month. She responded with the name of the area of the city she was living in and told him to pick a time and place to make it convenient for him. And so, she had only three days more to enjoy this texting romance, and she was ready to face the truth that it all was a game.

The next day he texted her set dinner time and the name of the best hotel near her house.

A day before, he texted her: "I am thrilled to meet you."

At eleven in the morning on the day of their dinner, he asked her to move dinner an hour later because he had to fly out later than he planned.

Two hours before set dinner time, he texted her: "In the air now!!".

Thirty minutes after, she texted him: "I guess I should get in the shower."

Two minutes after, he texted her: "Lol, will land in 5 minutes".

Ten minutes before dinner, she texted him that she was on her way. She was making a turn into the hotel's valet parking, thinking they never spoke on the phone. Game or not, she showed up.

Thirty seconds before dinner time, he texted her a picture of himself coming down in an elevator.

Take action. Nothing else counts.

Have you ever seen a TV commercial for Dos Equis beer's "The Most Interesting Man In the World"? The slogan is catchy, and it had nothing to do with their beer, but the real title of "The Most Interesting Man in the World" belongs to the mystery man with whom she had a four-hour dinner on the first evening of this month.

Six hours later, she returned to her apartment and texted him that she was home.

A minute after, he responded: "Good Night my beautiful."

Ten hours after, she woke up to a text message with the poem. Thirty sensual lines...events of those last few hours behind the doors of his hotel room. And a sudden electric lightning went through her mind and her physical body. She realized she finally found a man smarter than her, capable of fully dominating her sexually without causing her physical pain. Her Dream came true.

Make everyone benefit.

CHAPTER 16

Convenience

*"In his eyes woman like her was a golden ticket
to any event of life"*

Convenience was a big part of her life. She lived a ten minutes beautiful drive away from her workplace. Her son's A-list school was around the corner from their newly built modern apartment building. Her girlfriends lived no longer than twenty minutes away. The Pilates studio she started her days at was fifteen minutes away. And the city she lived in was filled with some of the most exciting people on the planet. Having an arrangement right here in her backyard would gift her a good amount of free time not spent in traffic getting somewhere else. She was waiting for the day to start one like that.

Seeking profiles with no pictures required a few extra steps before she would give a guy a chance to step into her perfect drama-free world. Some days she would spend the time to let them share their photos in different ways thru text messages or email. On other days she was busy, and she had no patience nor desire to waste her time on anyone playing hard to get.

His profile was not filled out. Fifty-seven years old, average build, average height, blond hair, blue eyes, million dollars a year income worth over hundred million net worth, married developer, and no photos. If he did not state his location as her little luxury town in his first message to her that day, she would pass his profile by, and that would be all. But he was a neighbor. He was that possible next-door convenient love affair she wanted to have. She messaged him back, asking for his phone number, and somehow, she forgot to log back into the site rest of that week.

He was waiting. He was polite, patiently waiting. It is an infrequent occasion in the online dating world. Men who have everything are used to getting things they want fast, and they get snappy and cut ties quickly if something is not happening fast enough for them. Two possible variations were about to happen in this case. There was something physically wrong with him, or he was brilliant. She loved to be proven wrong. It was a rare occasion, which she sincerely enjoyed. So, she texted him that she was ready to meet for a coffee. It was her first blind date of this arrangement type. And having that rare occasional coffee was a very lovely idea as well. She reached the point in her life when everything was nice, and it felt amazing.

The next day during her lunch break, she walked towards a cute neighborhood café. During the day, it was a busy spot for everyone having offices on that street to have their meetings or grab a quick bite with their kid after school. She never came here, she avoided her neighbors, and she did not like metal chairs with no cushions on them provided as sitting places in and out of the café. Little uncomfortable furniture detail like that could determine the result of this blind date she was about to have. If she was not comfortable sitting, her upbeat, cute personality could make a turn into something a bit too strong and hard to handle for the little gentlewoman everyone presumed her to be.

He arrived earlier than her; this might have been the first time she witnessed it happen in over thirty years. This man appeared to have all qualities of respect for other people's time. It is rare. And there was nothing wrong with him physically. She smiled and landed on a cold metal stool like it was upholstered with a silk French-style Renaissance chair.

Her almond milk latte tasted terrible. She was drinking it, not even noticing how bad it was. He was so careful with every word coming out of his mouth. He had one of those full mouths with big puffy lips. The last time she kissed someone like that was years ago. She loved older men and an older man with puffy lips. Mmm, lips like that on certain parts of her body were tempting.

He was intrigued by her; an hour passed, like two minutes. Neither of them wanted to go anywhere. She got up for him to admire her figure for switching his attention from having an intelligent conversation to a physical desire. It was there, but it was not how men looked at her. He looked at her much more than just a possible release from the everyday boredom of married life, and it was almost like he saw a whole universe inside her. It was similar to how a man looks at his business or his already successfully run projects. Her first husband always looked at her like that. She could see everyone like that herself. And to meet a man with this quality was a gift. The realization of this was more satisfying than anything else. More could happen between them in the future.

In the future, he drove three minutes from his house to her apartment in one of his numerous showoff cars. He would lay on her wave-shaped lounge chair in her living room and for two hours straight tell her about his relationships with his young girls-lovers he was trying to rescue from their meaningless lives one at a time, about lawsuits he won, new rare skins

Birkin bags he managed to get for his wife, another block he built to add to the Big Apple and all his other personal happenings. She listened and explained the behavior patterns of everyone he had trouble understanding. She always reminded him how wonderful he was as a person. Every week leaving her place, he reminded her he would marry her if something happened to his actual wife.

The way he looked at her was something special. He considered her a perfect wife and companion for any successful man. In his eyes, a woman like her was a golden ticket to any event in life.

Whenever she looked at his full puffy lips, she wondered if he would ever make a move to place them on her.

CHAPTER 17

The Accountant

*"Waking up in a great mood on a regular day and showing up
can gift you most wonderful encounters in your life"*

Pleasant surprises are the most wonderful when we don't
expect them. Waking up in a great mood on a regular day
and showing up can gift you the most beautiful encounters in
your life.

She enjoyed her life, and it had been two years since she
was single for the first time. She was a step ahead on her wish
list. She achieved all her plans fast and successfully. Most people keep working towards their dreams all their life, but not
her. She had to create new goals to make new wish lists. She
would have been considered a witch three hundred years ago
and most likely burnt alive. That is how different she was.

His Seeking profile belonged to a tall, beautiful athletic
man, the imaginary twin brother of Josh Duhamel. His smile
was childishly genuine, he was calm and confident. At forty-
nine, he did not look older than thirty-six. She felt how he is

just by looking at his photo. He had everything he needed. He did not need anyone or anything else. He had an agenda he was pursuing on Seeking Arrangement, but it had nothing to do with making an arrangement himself. He loved his life and was helping others learn to do the same. They both were on Seeking for the same reason, enriching their lives and creating happiness for everyone they encountered.

He asked her for her time and company to see her city. It was much less of what she hoped for by going on a date but doing something different and normal felt good today. She put on her flip-flops, left her wet hair air-dry, and she drove to the hotel he was staying at.

A very tall, beautiful male was standing in a large open lobby. He was at least two heads taller than her. As a sapiosexual, she rarely noticed men's outer beauty, but this was different. She could not take her eyes off him. She felt embarrassed and looked down. She was intimidated by him. His looks were smashing, plus she felt something else compelling inside him. She imagined this was how it felt, the same way men reacted in her presence. But this man showed no particular interest as a man in her as a woman.

They walked miles on her favorite touristic streets, and one conversation slowly led to another, which was beautiful. Strong September wind was playing with her hair. She was struggling to control it; he looked like he wanted to do something to help her, but he always kept his distance. A few times, she brushed the back side of her hand against the back side of his hand, and no reaction followed.

He invited her to dinner while passing by a busy Peruvian restaurant. She looked at him consuming a significant amount of food, followed by numerous glasses of alcohol. They talked about three hands full of places he lived growing up and all the pain he endured of adjusting to different countries, cultures, and societies while at it. Something had happened to him long ago, she could see it now in his eyes. His eyes were not tired from travel. He had a constant pain in his beautiful eyes. She wished she could change that for him. But there was no way she could climb that wall. Not tonight, for sure.

On the walk back to the hotel heat wave swallowed the city, and they made it back looking all sweaty. There was no indication of what he wanted to do next, and right before they reached the hotel's valet stand, he offered her to come up and continue to talk about everything else in the world they were both interested in. He had a fascinating set of talents, and if his looks did not hypnotize her, she would be convinced he was another government agent sent to interrogate her about men in her life.

The room was overly airconditioned. Being all wet from the outside heat and humid, she was almost shaking from the cold. He kept his distance all evening, she did not understand how it was possible to stay away from her, but she respected it. The hotel room was modern, with a glass shower wall overlooking an oversized bed and everything else. There was no privacy anywhere. She stepped into the shower room and took off her dress. The modern shower was an understatement, she pulled and turned, and no hot water was coming. He was standing on the other side of the room, looking at her water struggle. His fingers were typing something fast on his phone, but his eyes were on her.

"Help me," she said.

He crossed a large hotel room in three steps and stood by her side. He turned on the hot water with one handle turn and passed her a clean, dry towel. Hot water was running down her tan Pilates-toned body like a mighty waterfall. She was finally warmed up and refreshed.

She wrapped herself in a towel and jumped under the covers in his bed. She was not trying to provoke him, the room was still cold, and she struggled to keep herself warm. She was looking at him standing on the other side of the room looking at her. She could not read what he was thinking at all. She assumed at that moment he saw her as a child climbing into her parent's bed in the middle of the night to seek comfort. He looked like he did not know what to do with her in his room at all.

He turned off the shower light and turned on the water. It was not pitch black. Light from the room gave enough light in a shower for her to see him taking off his shirt and brushing his teeth. She was staring at his back silently while he looked at her in the mirror on the opposite side of the wall. The silence was heavy. There was no way she could predict what he would do next. Nothing in his face or body was giving out his thoughts or emotions. He took his pants off and stepped in into a steamy shower. She picked up her phone and returned to the S.A. website to re-read his profile and their brief conversation before the meeting. Maybe she missed something.

Nothing was wrong, but this was not planned. They both were the type of people who planned everything to the tiniest detail. He invited her to come up, he was not asking her to leave, and she wanted to stay.

He came out of the shower all wet with the towel wrapped around his waist. Standing right in front of her by the side of the bed, with his right hand, he was picking a Spotify list, and with his left hand, he was trying to fix a chain mixed up with another fabric string around his neck. She got up and stood on the bed next to him, helping him with the chain situation. Their eyes were at the same level. Soft jazz filled the room, and they kept looking at each other's eyes.

At that exact moment, she felt like gasping for air. His strong hands wrapped around her, and his mouth kissed her lips. He was confident, and he knew what he was doing. She felt it. He let her in. He did not want her body. He wanted all of her, including her mind and her soul. She leaned back and asked, "But how? I thought you were not into me."

And for the rest of the night, he did not stop telling her how much he wanted her when he saw her walking into the hotel lobby with her flip-flops on; and when strong winds were destroying her hair, and she seemed to have no care in the world about it.

He was passionately taking her repeatedly as nothing else existed during those hours. At times she screamed at the intensity of it. Her eyes rolled, and she was losing her sense of reality. He hungrily kissed every inch of her body like he was afraid he would never get to do it again once this night was over.

The night was over. He held her tight in his arms and fought her on her desire to leave him.

She always left. She always left to come back to him many times after. He was unbelievable in and out of bed.

Have you seen the movie *The Accountant*? Officially Ben Affleck's character was made up, but it wasn't. Unofficially her new lover's life was the base for that movie script. That is how special he was.

CHAPTER 18

Love and Politics

*"He showed up to lose any argument with her just
to win her over. She had no chances"*

Spending thirty years living an ordinary life by society's
standards and rules put her in a perfect position. She
succeeded at anything normal instantly. She was a wonderful
daughter, friend, girlfriend, wife, colleague, and mother. She
was so wonderful, even her mother-in-law loved her as her own
and maybe even more than her own. She was easily accepted
and liked by people of any race, religion, age, or status. Simply
put, everyone loved her, except she did not love herself.

Until she did, her whole world changed, and she lost most
people who loved her because she was no longer comfortable
with them. New people entered her life. Some stayed, exceptional people who did more, knew more, helped more, inspired
more, created more, and some were so much more you could
easily doubt they were human.

She was never bored. Her every day was filled with exciting things, people, lunches, dinners, and travel. But a constant desire to look and find more extraordinary never left the back side of her head. Every night she logged in to S.A. and read profiles of men trying to get her attention. Some days, maybe even weeks, no one exciting would come up. It was time to create the perfect storm herself and let someone in who was outside her criteria search.

His message was short and convincing. He saw her profile and knew she was the one he was looking for immediately. He wrote her he would agree to anything she wanted or needed because having her in his life would be priceless. Confidence coming from single sixty-nine years old, very accomplished good-looking man spiked all kinds of interests in her. And she agreed to meet for tea.

He was always twenty minutes late to everything of any importance. Major multitasker and mastermind. Former friend and partner to our dear president Donald Trump and many other fascinating individuals. American-born, all-traditional, people rights fighter showed up to their first date in Louis Vuitton sneakers, classic cut jeans, and a Lululemon sweater. He was funny, charming, and very agreeable. He showed up to lose any argument with her to win her over. She had no chance.

He cared for her in ways men cared for their women in old classic black and white beautiful movies. He swept her off her feet with his organizational skills and his personality. He was busy every second of the day, and he had her by his side at dinners with his family members, his partners, events, and other gatherings since day one. Day by day, she watched no one would question his authority. Everyone knew him, and everyone wanted his advice. She watched him and noticed something unique that she never figured out. He processed incoming information differently, and there were no proper words to explain it. He heard the information, but if he had to repeat it – it would come out as totally another new story. Still, his answer or an opinion on the originally incoming information would be right on point in the most innovative way! It was incredible. He was incredible.

Often, she found herself being just a part of his image. She was his companion and a number one date. She hugged and kissed him in public when she wanted to. He always put her on the pedestal above all in gatherings, but it often made her feel like a pedestal herself. She was in it for emotional interests, and she was interested in him and only him. She did not need to be around everyone else in his life. But there was almost no time just for the two of them. He noticed her mood change instantly, he would lean toward her and say, "Twenty minutes more. I will make it up to you."

And he always did. As soon as they were alone, he projected all his talents on her happiness. He was as good with her body as in all his businesses. And as soon as she was fully satisfied and tired, his attention switched back to saving the world with his incredible mind. He belonged to the world, and no one could ever compete with that.

Their rare weekend getaways he spent on conference calls or simply sleeping. She was a prisoner of hotel rooms and her own company with room service in front of the T.V. Did she want him? Yes. Did she need all of this? No.

It was a day when he expressed his desire for her to make an afford to make their Arrangement into a permanent relationship. He was offering her himself, not realizing he did not belong to himself to make an offer like that. He never figured out why she turned down an opportunity for this amazing public life with him.

CHAPTER 19

Young Sugar Daddy

*"Pride and joy filled her mind from realization
men like him still exist"*

Sugar Daddy. She never understood why someone in their right mind would want to be called like that. She had loved older men since she was fifteen. She dated and married men twice her age and older. And yes, all of them were smart and successful. She did not care to be called a Gold-digger, but no one in her life was allowed to be called a Sugar Daddy. She had only one Daddy; he was her father, and the most wonderful father a girl could wish for. Daddy was a sacred word for her; it meant love, respect, trust, and care. Not all older men she dated possessed all those qualities, she tried to go out with men her age as well, but that was a significant time-wasting. In her thirty-five years of life, she came across possibly ten exceptional male figures her age. She was done with going out with anyone under forty until a twenty-four years old young man made her an offer she could not refuse.

Many men eighteen and older contacted her with offers and showed interest. She read each of their profiles and never responded. Trust fund kids, young tech moguls, T.V. show actors. All of them had an ego, and they partied. At twelve years old, she had her first job creating advertisement flyers for a local nightclub in the little town she grew up in. Having had access to fun since her teen years, she was done with nightclubs and parties by eighteen. You could never meet her there unless her modeling jobs were held at clubs or lounges.

His profile had no picture, and he was ten years younger than her, tall and skinny by description, college degree educated, no wife, no kids, and no hobbies. His profile said he had just sold his med-tech company for millions and was moving into her city. He wrote her asking if she could do a restaurant tour for him and he would very much appreciate a good conversation while at it. She was surprised by a grown man's approach from twenty-four years old. She agreed and completely forgot to ask him to send her his picture.

She made a dinner reservation in a nice, not known to many, artisan-style restaurant on the twenty-fifth floor of a hotel he was staying at. There were large modern artworks on every wall. She loved art. Her apartment looked like an art gallery. She was looking at the piece where celebrities' faces were mixing one with another depending on what angle you stood to the art piece. Somewhere between Justin Timberlake melting into Miley Cyrus, the elevator door opened, and a tall young man dressed in all black started walking toward her. He had Asian features, big brown eyes, and puffy pink lips that stood out on a skinny face. He smiled, and a genuine full mouth of white teeth lighted up the room. It was apparent he was nerdy, but how he was dressed gave out a piece of knowledge in class and style. His Italian leather pointy-toe narrow dress shoes were a rare occasion to see men wear in the United States.

An hour into dinner conversation about everything in the world, she realized he was one of those young men who would be part of the group making our world better. At a young age, he knew exactly what he wanted, and he was capable of creating magnificent innovations. This Harvard dropout, at first not supported by his traditional family, took an idea, built it, and turned it into millions of dollars. That was inspiring. He did not party. He traveled to hard to get non touristic places, he shopped high-end real estate, he read books, and he socialized with older interesting people.

She asked him if he realized she was ten years older than him. In response, he smiled and said, "I was looking for older. I would die if you suggested hitting the club or anything like that".

So here he was, her preferred man in a much younger version. Pride and joy filled her mind from the realization men like him still exist.

She followed him to his hotel room out of curiosity. Could that be he also was as mature in bed as outside of it? Did he know how and where to kiss and touch? Would he dominate or follow her?

They started to kiss as soon as the hotel room's door was closed. The room was pitch black. He did not seem shy at all. She leaned back, stepped away from him, turned on the light, and entered the bathroom. The shower got quickly hot, and the pressure was perfect. She was refreshed, warm, and excited. A fluffy white hotel towel barely covered her body.

He was fully undressed, half lying, half sitting in bed under covers. Her towel dropped to the floor to his sound of: "Wow." She sat on top of him, guessing what he would like to play with first, but he was frozen and not moving. She leaned down and started to kiss his mouth. He responded, but not as confident as they just entered the room a few minutes earlier. It began to feel like they were two teens just starting to explore the adult world. He was not shy but did not know what he could do or how. He was not asking for directions. He was unsure. Looking briefly into his eyes, she saw he was not on top of his game here. There were no other options, it was her play here, and she played as she wanted. Half an hour later, they both landed at the finish line simultaneously, and he looked like the happiest young man on Earth.

He returned to his project, and she returned to her older men.

CHAPTER 20

Bad Boys

*"The intensity of everything else he did to her, for her,
took her to unimaginable high, and once you are there,
reality as you know it loses its realism and you are never no longer
the same. And for the rest of your life you are looking
for your way back up there"*

Bad boys. Successful mature men with young Mickey Rourke's looks and The Godfather's attitude. There are so few of them, and they are always busy enjoying their lives. Full of confidence and sex drive, creative and dominant in a most gentle way. You can never remember intimacy with men like that. It is a magnificent blur. They take you, and you no longer belong to yourself until they choose to let you go. They lift you, twist you and turn you. You feel weightless, fully taken, penetrated in ways you could not imagine happening to you. Men like that are magicians. They are rare and should be preserved and cloned because their power and energy are priceless.

His profile popped out in her Seeking suggestions multiple times. Every time she clicked on it – she received a simple visual orgasm. One must be blind not to realize what kind of man was before her. He was the worst in the greatest way. Her heart rate would go off in her healthy body, and her vision would blur. She was secretly in an arrangement with him already. He was The sexual perfection, a human sex machine with a brain, many creative talents, and multiple zeros in his bank account. They would never talk. Men like him are not able to listen. They talk – you listen. They are like hypnotizing snakes luring you closer just by being in your presence or just looking at you from the online picture format. Men like that get off on making their women lose their minds, and that feeling is one of the most powerful she ever felt after love.

His pinned location was her home zip code, they were neighbors in real life. She stopped contacting men herself months before, as there is nothing better than being a target to an experienced hunter. One of these days, he would find her, and she could not wait for that to happen.

It must have been months before he wrote her. He asked: "What and when?". He spoke the impatient language of "I see it, I want it, I get it, I have it."

They lived in the same universe, and they spoke the same language regular people didn't know. The mad universe, consisting only of highs, tenses, and breathiness, where you speak in looks, lip bites, high pulses, and chest rises. She was waiting, and she knew what was coming her way. But he did not know that she knew, and he did not expect to find someone who spoke the same language. He offered her the most normal meeting to start with, daytime lunch in Soho House private club, and she said: "No".

Weeks after, he texted her his congratulations on the Christmas holidays. She responded with "Thank you" only.

January eight of the next year, he texted her: "How do you want it?".

A text with her address and a time the next day came into his phone screen seconds after.

At the exact right time, she opened her front door wearing a lacy silk robe over her pulsating naked body. Her long blond hair was still wet after the shower.

He was tall, lean, and in fantastic shape. It is not known if he ever worked out. It seemed he was built that way naturally. Toned tan beautiful body. His loose white linen shirt was half open, his chest was one of those your hands go subconsciously for. A touch of magic. Short-fitted white Ralph Lauren shorts on long muscular legs. He stepped over her doorway, grabbed her by the waist with his right arm lifting her up, and everything else lost its clearness. Somehow, he kissed her mouth and carried her into her bedroom like he knew which way to go. When her weightless body landed on her bed, she was naked. No sight of her close and no idea when exactly that happened. She was losing it. She could not focus or control herself, him, or anything.

He took his clothes off. It was much more than she hoped for. She shook her head, almost silently said "No," and crawled to her bed headboard. He smiled, grabbed one of her long legs he could easily reach, and pulled her towards him.

In some countries, it could be considered rape, witchcraft, or even being kidnapped by aliens. He had her, and he owned her. For about thirty minutes, he fully possessed her body and soul. They did not know each other, but he ate her like she was his favorite thing to eat. Her eyes rolled so deep. She could not open them. She felt his fingers penetrating all of her so easily, like he was the one who designed her body just for himself from scratch. His fingers were long, thick, soft, demanding, powerful, and gentle. She climaxed so many times in a row the feeling became constant. She was lost in his lust for her.

His mouth made its way up her body until he reached her ear and whispered: "Are you ready?".

She was not, but he was not really asking. The intensity of everything else he did to her, for her, took her to an unimaginable high, and once you are there, reality as you know it loses its realism, and you are never no longer the same. And for the rest of your life, you are looking for your way back up there, to men like her new Mr. Intense neighbor.

CHAPTER 21

Body Pleasures

"She had a talent to feel everything so deeply"

We are all so different and so similar. But the truth is all she had in her – you have in you. You just have not discovered it yet. She chose every event in her life. She chose her people, and she chose her experiences. She made lots of mistakes, and she saved lots of lives along the way. She had one simple desire, as you all do. She wanted to love with all her heart. She was looking for that person to love among all the ones who lived their lives in full as she did. Seeking was her door to those one-of-a-kind people. Men. Men of Seeking Arrangement. It is where she found her biggest love to this date, and she managed to fall in love with another while still longing to be with her biggest love. She had a talent for feeling everything so deeply.

Every man she let into her life was well chosen, and everyone had a chance to complete her. Many tried, and more will try until she finds The One or settles for someone comfortable.

And until she does, she will open her life to the most incredible people with the most amazing life stories.

Every week she had lunch with her very close male friend and his uncle. She and her male friend had an affair many years ago. After that ended, they became fantastic friends. He was as close as a family to her. They would lunch at one of the town's most popular and busy restaurants. People arrived in their Bugattis, Rolls Royse, Bentleys, McLarens, and Ferraris, and the valet line was endless. Italian food was good and fast. People were fashionable, rich, and famous. Their table always attracted attention. Restaurant owners were bringing out ordered dishes themselves. Her loud happy laugh was turning heads. Her outfits and jewelry drew all eyes. A beautiful young woman could have been her lunch companions' granddaughter, maybe a great-granddaughter or daughter. But occasionally, she would stroke the face of one of the men with her gentle touch, and only blind would not notice the amount of love those two shared for each other deep inside them.

She saw her new Mr. Intense neighbor often lunching alone at that busy restaurant. He was always eating alone. Sometimes he would briefly converse with people sitting at the table next to his. He never smiled. This man and the man she had in her apartment weeks before were not the same person. Very different. Scary different. He was happy and excited and non-stop smiling with her. And without her, he looked older, colder, bitter, rough, and grumpy. He has not contacted her since they have connected. She never called or texted men first. But every night before falling asleep, she wished to reconnect with him.

That day she watched him finish his lunch and leave the restaurant, passing right by the table she was lunching at. He was walking and looking directly at her. Not stopping, he smiled and nodded, saying a silent 'Hi' to her. An hour later, she got a text from him: "My house. Black lingerie, stockings, high heels. Toys".

That evening she was taking an elevator down to her car dressed precisely as requested, and for the first time, she wished not to run into any of her family-friendly building neighbors. No, she was not embarrassed. Half of her building's male population somehow already found her on Instagram, and they were profoundly watching everything she chose to display. Her army of silent followers. Neighbors' wives did not like her as a single mother neighbor, an obvious MILF, they rarely said "Hi" to her on the building premises, and she understood them. She was younger, and she was beautiful. She was free and happy. She was the one they wanted to be or to look like, she was a blemish in their eyes, and that blemish did not plan to move anywhere else. Imagine seeing her in a tight black leather mini skirt barely covering the lacy upper part of the sheer silky black stockings, a black lace camisole top floating over her beautiful natural breasts, and tall black high heels toped the picture. She had a large black Chanel leather travel case filled with a few of her favorite toys. She was excited to play, and she was brave this time.

Passing the security gate, she arrived at his driveway. He was waiting for her at his front door entrance. She got out of her car and, with her million dollars walk, started to walk towards him. Her mind had already left this world. Her mind was rising to the stars imagining laying under his energetic body, pulsating and dissolving in absolute pleasure. Would it be more than thirty minutes this second time?

He was smiling all teeth.

"You are the first guest in my house," he said.

And she has awoken from her dreamy sexual state. He was opening up to her. He was talking about himself and his life. And that was something she did not expect from him.

He cooked a lovely dinner, lamb chops, crispy roast potatoes, and guacamole cherry tomatoes. The food tasted amazing. He showed her around the house and the backyard.

The backyard was his happy place. Thick walls of tall green bushes surrounded him. It was just him and one iguana he friended. Sometimes you could hear the neighbors, but no one could see thru the thick green walls.

He seemed happy with everything around him. She was looking at him and could not take her eyes off him. There was a literary light coming from within him. She wondered if he knew that about himself.

He was born and raised in Manhattan in a mobster family, led by an example of a fantastic mother running a huge liquor empire and a consistently supportive, caring father, whom everyone was carefully afraid of. He had a sister murdered by her boyfriend psychopath. He had a worldwide retail business and a family of his own somewhere in the other part of the world. If you Googled his name, there are endless chats about his personal life. Actual men were trying to contact him, asking him to refuse their wives and girlfriends' sexual favors. He was a character in a category of his own. In a few years, you will find his autobiography in bookstores, but tonight, he belonged just to her. And it was way over thirty minutes.

Sex was out of this world. He was a wild animal when it came to that. He knew his way with her toys like they were his own. The intensity of body pleasure she had experienced that night was a first for her. He pushed her beyond her limits. If she were married, her husband definitely would join that online list of men begging to leave their women be.

CHAPTER 22

Falling Back in Love

*"And a man, trying to forget one woman from his past,
is very persuading in loving new one in his present"*

Often, we meet people with very traditional lives, and we assume we can predict what they think or what they will do next. We enjoy their company, but we are not excited enough because people living traditional lives are not big risk-takers, and they don't do much of borderline anything exciting with their lives. She saw traditional in a more advanced way than society did, but still, it was traditional. Her type of traditional people traveled places on hot air balloons and ate at restaurants with twenty-five tasting menu items described only as emojis. They had young lovers, and stay-at-home wives they were not in a rush to spoil in any way. They would buy thousands of dollars of art to hang in a house, but they would not spend a few thousand on an anniversary gift their spouse dreams of. Silly things, silly priorities. No wonder love leaves relationships like that.

His profile had a private hidden photo, forty-nine years old married man with college-age children, a degree in finance, and lots of love for art, good food, travel, and cultured entertainment. He was easy to communicate with. He was in great shape and handsome. According to his profile's record, he registered just days before and, not having much experience in site life on the Seeking Arrangement platform, he was very polite and welcoming.

They met for coffee the next day, half the distance between their locations. She came early and parked right by the back entrance to Starbucks. She saw him pull into the parking lot minutes after her, and she watched him looking for parking for at least ten minutes. The unavailability of parking did not make him change a muscle in his face, which was a good sign.

He was charming and very calm, confident, and sure about what he wanted. Being married all his life, he mentioned he loved his wife very much.

He recently had a love affair. He had run into a young student a few years prior and was very fond of the girl. He put her up in a lovely brand-new apartment in an office district block away from his office. That girl stopped doing anything and lived her life to accommodate his almost daily but brief visits. Occasionally they took "work trips" to the islands together, and he was happy until one day, his young girl met a young man with no prospects, and she left her mature, stable, successful unavailable lover all alone in his loveless life.

Months into that affair, he considered leaving his family and starting a new one with his new young protégé. It is great he did not. Love is great, but one should never marry another who is with him not for the right reasons.

He said he loved his wife very much. She did not believe it. He loved a young girl who left him, he was very collected in his feeling, but the intonation of the words he used did not lie. He was hurt and he believed a new love affair would fix all his problems.

She was the right woman for the task. Turning lives around and saving marriages was one of her specialties. They agreed on an arrangement, and she took him as a project. They had lots of interests in common, she was excited to see where all this could go and for how long. And a man, trying to forget one woman from his past, is very persuading in loving a new one in his present. Attention, care, and passion skyrocket in situations like this. Finishing up her coffee, she imagined how he would unleash all his manhood on her. She smiled, and they picked an afternoon to spend together later in the week.

Their weekly affair lasted a couple of months. They would lock themselves up on a higher floor in one of the hotels downtown. She took the second half a day off work, and he, as an executive at a major bank, had an option of a very long lunch absence from the office. He was able to dissolve himself in her once they were physically intimate. He was passionate and giving for a good two hours at a time.

But before or after bizarre things would happen, it was hard to say if they were coincidences or well-planned—at least some of them.

She would look out of the hotel room's window down the pool and enjoy the sunlight. He would stand beside her and point at the exact apartment his young mistress used to share with him across the street overlooking the same hotel pool.

She would go to other Caribbean islands exploration with her son, get another major sunburn and text him a photo of her new funny tan lines. He would text back with a picture he took of his former young mistress in the same sunburned situation.

Sometimes they would meet at the hotel with its private beach, and she would lay on top of him on a single tanning bed and talk about everything in the world. And he would point at a place nearby and tell her his former little lover works there now.

It was very unusual. He adored her. He missed her while they were apart. He brought her thoughtful gifts from travel with his family. And he always could not wait to see her again, but in addition to his wife, they had a foursome because his young lover from the past was always "with them."

His young lover looked like a girl next door, with mid-length dark hair and a slim build. She did not work out. She was not particularly beautiful in any way. The young girl did not work, and she had no interests. A blank. Raw material to build something regular out of it. And he loved that person. He would not admit it, but she saw it in him. And she felt sad for him.

He was planning to take his wife away on a romantic trip for Valentine's Day. He had a plan to reconnect with her in all ways possible and turn around their marriage into a new honeymoon stage. She listened to him, and nothing she could say. She has never met men who succeeded at a task like that. And she did not believe it was possible to achieve.

Four days after, he called her to say goodbye.

He did it. He fell back in love with his wife of over two decades. He was starting over with his own family. He sounded happy and excited. She was very happy for him but could not shake the feeling of something wrong. No, she was not jealous, competitive, or possessive. She knew she would get a replacement for him in the next hour or so. But her intuition rarely lied to her. She could not believe he could revive his feelings just like that on demand. Finally, she found something interesting about him.

Months later, she was walking with her son on the most popular touristic boulevard in the city and saw him. He was walking with an older version of his young little ex-mistress. He was holding his wife's hand and looked peaceful and happy.

His wife could have been an aged twin of the young girl he was recently in love with. She had some grey hair mixed with her dark hair. She was skinny but not in shape. Flats, jeans, relaxed, over-washed t-shirt, and no make-up. She did not smile and looked bothered. It was beautiful to see them like that.

CHAPTER 23

Love and Distance

*"Distance and Time must be only factors to define
feeling of love for one or another"*

Love and Distance. Distance and Time must be the only factors to define feelings of love for one or another. She believed if you love someone truly, you will carry that feeling with you thru anything. It had nothing to do with being in love or being passionate, wanting to be in a relationship, an arrangement, or living together happily ever after. Love like that existed in its universe; it was healthy, and it was beautiful. You could feel it whenever that particular person crossed your mind or in the hours you decided to spend together. You can live in Key West, Florida, and he could live in Perth, Australia. And yet, the love you shared did not feel that distance or time spent apart.

His Seeking profile showed three men playing some unknown to her sport together. He was forty-nine years old, British look, beyond athletic, well-educated, and traveled a lot. He was currently in her city and departing the following morning. It did not make much sense to write him back or make time to see him, but something was pulling her towards this man. She responded, and they started all day texting adventure. He was funny and very well put together. A perfect gentleman with an exquisite sense of humor she was not able to identify right away. A few hours into their online conversation, they had to meet. And he had no time.

Her car pulled into the driveway of the hotel he was staying a few minutes past ten in the evening. She was tired, and she could not understand her actions, but she needed to be there. She obeyed that feeling pulling her towards the unknown. This possible arrangement did not make any sense. This might be the only time they ever have a chance to meet and be together for a couple of hours. Their locations did not match in any way possible. But she felt like she was reconnecting with someone very dear to her. She could not explain it, but it felt like they already knew each other. It felt like they have already spent a whole life together.

His Uber arrived a few minutes past her arrival. He did not look a year older than thirty. Full on energy and positivity. He was one of those she could not predict or read him. He was far more advanced as a human being than her. He knew who he was and what he wanted to do. And at that moment, she realized he was here for her, not the opposite, like she liked to believe. He was here to save her and lead her to the better version of herself she always worked towards being. And the moment their eyes met, they both understood they were a part of something bigger than all of this.

He put his sport coat over her bare shoulders and grabbed her hand. He led her through the lobby to an elevator. They did not look at each other anymore, and they did not talk. She had a silent confusion in emotions and feelings inside her. All this did not feel real. Real always has a slight variation of some uncertainty or little detail she did not like or disapprove of. But her hand felt perfectly warm and comfortable in his. At this particular moment, he felt closer to her than her ex-husbands ever did.

His hotel room was enormously big. She sat on the couch before the T.V. and took off her shoes. She watched him ordering room service and looking for a T.V. remote. His posture and body language were of a young boy. He was childish and playful. He sat on the opposite side of the couch, and they talked. They talked about work event that brought him into town and the long dinner with his employees he tried to finish as early as possible. He told her about his family and his lifestyle. He was married more to an airplane seat than to his wife. Real-life traveler, spending more hours in the air than on the ground. Tech inventor and finance expert. A rare combination of an athlete and a nerd.

They rented a movie, and she watched him devouring his pasta on the other side of the couch. He finished eating and disappeared into a shower.

She got up and walked over to a window. Downtown looked incredible at night. If she did not know where she was, you could imagine the Manhattan skyline and have no doubt you were there. Millions of stars were shining bright on her. The weather will be fantastic tomorrow.

She grabbed a blanket and walked back to a couch. This time she lay down and continued to watch a movie. He came out of the bathroom with wet hair and wearing full-size pajamas. He magically made his way behind her and hugged her from behind. They watched another 40 minutes of the movie comfortably lying down together, hugging. Not once did he move or move his arm. He did not try to touch her or kiss her. She looked back at him several times to understand if he had fallen asleep, but he was fully awake.

The movie was over, and the day caught up to her. She was tired and practically falling asleep. His body was in three different time zones in the last 48 hours. She could only imagine how he was still awake and functioning. So, she decided to sleep for an hour and drive home after.

She got in his bed, not taking her dress off. He laid down facing her right next to her and hugged her. And they fell asleep instantly. She did not know how many minutes or hours had passed, but at some point, their lips found each other. His lips found every inch of her body, they have lost time, but they found each other that late evening.

She just loved him, and he made trips across the world to spend just a few hours, and sometimes days, with her. They took beach walks and steamy showers, she showed him her city, and he introduced her to his team. They barely communicated when they were apart, but no one was as close together as when he was occasionally next to her.

CHAPTER 24

Privacy

*"It is a terrifying feeling of the unknown, because every step
you take in someone else's private world, you end up
not knowing what exactly your foot will touch"*

There are people among us living in the same environment
and society, sleeping, eating, walking, and breathing, but
they are not like us. They never fit in, and they choose not
even to try. They are beautiful, attractive, and successful. Still,
no one knows about them because some people don't interact
with the outside world. She did not believe it was possible until
she entered a private world like that. It is a terrifying feeling of
the unknown because, with every step you take in someone
else's world, you do not know what your foot will touch.

Every time Seeking profile with age younger than forty
messaged her, she responded with the list of things she had
to have in a possible arrangement relationship. Younger men
usually did not have enough consideration even to process that
a woman could be so straightforward and demanding in her

first response to a stranger. They would text back something offensive or aggressive and move on. This way, she avoided the possibility of wasting time on someone who was "not her person." Occasionally some manipulator would play along in her game and disappear right before the meeting. And just a few out of hundreds simply said yes to all her required nonsense. Those men were exactly the type she liked to surround herself with. Pandora's box in a human form!

His pictures were a Salvador Dali-type shirtless young man holding his surfboard, Gatsby overdressed to impress a gentleman, and a shirtless good-looking relaxed man lying on his back on a black leather couch. Three diffcrent personalities in one person, she wondered how many more other variations he had in him. He was skinny but all lean muscles. Few rare-looking tattoos, a collection of diving watches, and natural stones Tibetan style bead jewelry.

His phone number was unregistered, and nothing indicated that he was honest and serious about creating an arrangement. They planned a dinner date for next week, and to her surprise next day, she happened to see him walking outside on a little street with local restaurants in his neighborhood where she had just had an early dinner with her girlfriends. She did not imagine it. It was him, wearing a similar Gatsby-style jacket, dark blue Adriano Goldstein pants, and custom-made Italian dress shoes. This situation took another turn. Deep inside, she was convinced he would disappear hours before their dinner because he was not real, but there he was in flesh and blood.

They texted a few times on the day they had planned to have dinner. Everything was good and seemed beautiful. She parked her car next to his building, and a minute later, he walked towards her with a rose in his hand. He wore a black T-shirt under another dressy-looking jacket. Usually, her beautiful dresses, high heels, and overpriced purses attracted attention to her and her dates, but tonight he outshined her. A rose was a nice touch. He was romantic.

The restaurant he picked was two blocks away on the same local little street she saw him another day, they walked, and he greeted every valet, hostess, older woman selling flowers, and homeless people by their names. It seemed very nice how friendly he was to people in general. They sat at the restaurant bar, and the bartender asked if he would have the usual.

He seemed very normal and pleasant. He loved old classic movies and art. All his life stories were about his teen years and twenties and nothing after that—a complete blank from the twenties to almost fifty. The age in his profile was incorrect, but nothing in his look gave it out. He did not look older than thirty. He did not own a car, and he never left the perimeter of five blocks around the building he was staying at. He surfed every morning, and he made sure he watched every sunset. He spends hurricane season in the South of France and around the coast of Spain. He let out a few details about his parents and nothing else.

She still had a feeling he was not a real person. The way he was and lived was out of touch with reality. He was very confident in himself and everything he was doing. She was curious to find out more.

They had a nice dinner, an easy conversation, and she decided to go for it. They walked back to his apartment. It was a beautiful breezy night. You could feel and smell the ocean nearby. A stranger walked towards them, stopped right in front of them, and started to tell her new date how he was glad to see him and that he just spoke about him with so and so. Her new date froze in silence, he did not say a word to a stranger, and they silently continued to walk towards the apartment building he lived at. And she could not stop the feeling of oddness in this whole new contact she made. It was thrilling, not scary. She kept waiting for the moment of some clarity, but she never found it over the many months they had spent together in the future.

His place was dark. He must have had hundreds of candles lit up all over the apartment. He smoked indoors, and everything had a constant smell of cigarettes. She did not like dark places, smoke, and candles. All of it had an impression of some sort of ritual on her. She walked around, and she realized there was no bedroom. At that moment, she decided not to ask any more questions.

One of the rooms had four yoga chairs of different shapes. She assumed he slept there.

There was a couch in the living room, and she sat down there as it seemed the only normal thing in his apartment. She sat down, and she froze. It was one of the rare moments in her life when she could not predict what would happen next.

He did not talk about his work, he seemed to have no friends, and he never had a family of his own. The old classic movie was always playing in the background on tv, and an absolutely different style of music played every time they stayed in.

He was a perfect lover. He was gentle and demanding at the same time. He was making sure she had in times more pleasure before he did. Every time she was walking in blind into some scenario he well thought off. He had new sets of lingerie prepared for her. He knew all the sensual positions in and out of the couch and around his yoga chairs. He had fresh flowers for her, and he always made her house-made herbal tea from his own garden he built on his top-floor balcony. She watched his every move outside of sex. She could never shake the feeling something was off here. But she never found it.

A few weeks into their arrangement, she commented on him not having a bedroom. He stopped smoking, and he asked her: "Are you sure you want to see my bedroom?".

She looked confused. She had been in this place multiple times, and there was no bedroom. He took her hand and led her to his bedroom. How this was possible, she did not know. A room appeared. It was dark. It did have a king-size bed. And it had soft handcuffs on both sides of the bed's headboard. She felt confused. Nothing was predictable about this guy. Everything about him and everything he was up to was different from anything she had ever experienced.

"Do you trust me?" he asked.

She did not, but he never made her feel anything uncomfortable physically. He was gentle and careful. He always asked her for feedback if he was going hard. So, she nodded.

He stepped into his walk-in closet, which she had never seen before, and returned with a real blindfold. The blindfold was soft and silky. It gave an illusion of intrigue, but she still could see if she chose to open her eyes.

She finally laid down in his bed. He cuffed her wrists, but to her surprise, she could take her hands off it any second. All this was an illusion. Nothing was restricting her from leaving at any second. He got up and left the room. A minute after, she heard the buzzing of an electric toy. He was pleasuring her only for an endless amount of time that night, taking her to heights she rarely reached in her version of ordinary life. It was the only night she had a chance to enjoy it, and for the remaining many months, they enjoyed each other's company, she secretly dreamed of returning to his bedroom, but he never took her there again.

CHAPTER 25

One of a Kind

"Being together with one of a kind is priceless"

Have you ever felt like you are one of a kind in the whole universe? From the moment we are born, we tend to try to belong, to fit into society, to do and to be normal. And while you do that, you know you are definitely doing the right thing, the right thing for What in order to get somewhere, but not for Whom. She tried to fit in all her life. The harder she tried – the less happy she was. Pleasing people was her specialty. She loved people, all people. And they loved to be loved by her. Most of the time, they used it, and she let it happen until she did not anymore. And the day she decided to turn her hamster wheel in an opposite direction, her value went to the roof. The line to get to her was endless, and the ones who stood next to her - never wanted to share her for a second with anyone else. Being together with one of a kind is priceless.

He contacted her a couple of times, she was aware of it. But he had too much information to read in his Seeking profile and his messages to her, and she simply was no longer interested in putting in any afford-to-read thoughts on paper of any men she did not know. The man was not giving up. Even at a simple overlook of his details, she knew he had nothing she would be interested in, but he kept writing her.

Seasonal traffic in her favorite city was awful. You could be sitting on the same block for half an hour. Living in one of the most popular areas of town did not help this situation either. On the in-traffic-sitting afternoon like that, she opened her Seeking app and she gave all unanswered communication a try.

His profile belonged to a forty-nine-year-old athletic-looking man with a posture and a build for a National Hockey League. Another forty-nine years old. It is not even funny, a popular dating statistics number, but it is pathetic. An interesting detail was the fifty million dollars net worth, with over a million a year made. Athletic and smart. Or someone must have had a great financial adviser per the completion of his athletic career. You can see she was annoyed, and the current traffic hold-up was affecting her judgment of building a profile of possibly a great man she was never going to meet.

He had grown children. He was married before, well-educated, well-traveled, and good-looking, with farms, ranches, absolutely different businesses, houses in other countries, and various boats. He was almost perfect for her, but one detail. He had a long-term girlfriend, and he was looking for someone else very nice to put in his sandwich. A beautiful all-natural woman was sitting next to him in his pictures. Woman was beautiful and seemed genuinely nice.

She had no bad feelings for women, but she was not excited by them. Many years ago, she met someone beautiful in and out. They almost looked like twins. It lasted three weeks, and it was more than enough to realize women were not her thing. So, she would never return to that again, even if she was bored, but she was never bored. Even sitting in traffic on the same block for thirty minutes would not get her feeling bored for a second. Annoyed yes, bored – no.

A Canadian gentleman with a beautiful life, muscular body, and most likely a beautiful mind was offering her a variety of scenarios he was good with to meet her. And none of those scenarios spiked any interest in her. And being extremely honest and straightforward, she responded with a hard "No" to all his offers.

A minute after, he responded with a surprisingly short message: "I will do what you want."

Three days after, she stood by the entrance to a charming family-owned Italian restaurant next to her house, and she watched him a block away, crossing the street and walking towards her. Hundred percent former professional hockey player. Muscular, solid legs and that particular walk. She could walk like that, too, after riding a horse for an hour. To put humor aside, he was a beautiful man with the manners of a gentleman. He was intelligent and funny. After thirty minutes into the Italian dining experience, he found himself in a tricky situation. He understood he could no longer be honest with his long-term girlfriend because he unexpectedly fell for someone out of this world he was not expecting to meet.

And just like that, one of North America's most eligible bachelors forgot about his plans for sexual adventures, and he melted into a fallen teenager with one agenda – to please the object of his desire.

His boat was parked in the busiest marina in the center of the city below a few of the most populated high-end condominiums. It was late, and his staff was sleeping. It was a weekday, and no apartments above them had any parties. You could hear the ocean and cars flying by on the nearby causeway if they did not talk.

He kissed her when she crossed from a dock into a boat and put her shoes down. She was climbing to the upper dock, undressing herself along the way. Here and there, he was quick enough to plant a kiss on her shoulder or her knee or her feet. Up top, she got into the captain's high chair and put her feet on the navigation displays in front of her. They were on display for anyone who stepped out that late night to take a breath of fresh air. She hoped someone was watching because she was in the mood to display a wild rodeo.

Former hockey players have great stamina.

He lasted for months; their wild rodeo coasted him his long-term relationship. But don't you worry, submissive women always return to their masters once their masters are done serving their one and only Miss.

CHAPTER 26

The Real Husband

"He walked into her apartment and told her he never done this before. She smiled. Aren't they all never done this before?!"

The beautiful lives of celebrities and tv personalities dictate some of us standards of living and standards to seek in our relationship. And not many understand what is staged and what is real. She always preferred real. When Real Housewives of "her town" came out on TV, it was entertaining to watch all the pretense of the lives of women she was familiar with. Some were incredibly brave to show their real personal lives. It was not about smart or beautiful. It was about going raw with all of yourself into the world of perfection and setting a standard high for anyone else. And some were acting. This part was tricky because those women were very interesting individuals themselves. Still, instead of opening up and sharing their uniqueness, they chose to become someone else on TV for millions of people watching them. But the most interesting was their husbands and their life partners rarely appeared in episodes. Some were quick to show up and disappear, some played along and barely could hold their amusement of their Real Housewives acting, and some men chose to stay themselves at all times. And there was only one she could not take her eyes off when he rarely came to light.

Occasionally she saw him crossing the street where she got her Starbucks coffee or her nails done that day. Other times she looked across the room, and his profile appeared at another table in one of the famous restaurants she dined in. He did not belong to this time, he was from another era where gentleman still existed, when men dressed appropriately, and manners were appreciated. He always looked calm and very well put together. Stylish European man in the middle of American expression of freedom in everything. Nothing else she knew about him, and there was no reason to dig deeper since he belonged to someone else. Until the day he contacted her on Seeking.

She looked at his private pictures, and she could not believe it. His beautiful face, skinnier athletic body, real first name, and completely different style in clothes, but this was the man she used to admire from her TV screen, the front seat of her auto, and distant tables at different restaurants. It was customary to her when all her dreams and desires came true, but this was undoubtedly a gift from the universe she loved so much, and the universe loved her back!

She pretended she had no idea who he was, and she responded in the same manner as she did to anyone else. This time she let him dictate the arrangement he wanted. Maybe to him, it was what it was supposed to be, but to her – she was going to dive into her long overdue mental love affair she was already in for a couple of years. They went over the details of no drama, no interference in personal lives while not together, the expected frequency of meetings, and phone numbers exchange. And he disappeared.

Every time she texted him to schedule a time together, he was out of town. She was out of town more often than anyone else she knew, but every time she was in town – he was not. He was disclosing his locations, hotels, restaurants, bars, work projects, and people he was with. He wanted to share, but he was sharing his texts, not himself. And she was only interested in real in-person thing. He was here for the feeling, not the knowing. The more he shared his everyday life, the less and less he reminded her of the man she watched on TV occasionally. This same person seemed divided into two different personalities, and not one of them she could get to see in person.

She deleted his contact and moved on to the Christmas holidays, overseas travel, and making memories with her favorite guy in the whole world, her almost grown little man, her son. By the time she got back into her usual beautiful life, she had a lineup made of a businessman, a banker, a doctor, a politician, and her ex-boyfriend as options for personal, romantic amusement.

And once all five dates were scheduled, she gladly welcomed an idea of a new arrangement or maybe even a comeback relationship. The first work week of the new year was busy with work and scheduling ten thousand different things. She barely slept, and she was physically and mentally exhausted. But she was happy, she lived a life of her dreams, a life where all her dreams came true hourly, if not daily. And that is when one of those unfinished-business dreams reappeared as a text from a number she erased weeks ago.

They both were in the same town; his work was three blocks away from her apartment, and she had an hour and a half before she was supposed to be at work.

She watched his classic car pull into her driveway. Dressed like a teenager in trendy keds, skinny jeans, and a tight white t-shirt, the object of her desire was making his way to her intercom. To her, not having sex for weeks added to the anticipation of his arrival another level of "want." He was the exact psychological type of man her subconscious mind was drawn to. Not knowing how his body would feel against hers, his smell and his taste, she knew they both would end up in space once she opened her front door.

He walked into her apartment and told her he had never done this before. She smiled. Aren't they all never done this before?! Ah, men.

She had not seen him this close yet, calm and confident in person, and he was comfortable where he was. He looked at her as if she was the eighth wonder of the world. He was happy he made it here. He was not trying to figure her out but was here to love her. Love her for minutes or longer if they let themselves go that far. He was the same type as her. They both were made out of pure unpretended pleasure. She was silent for a change, and she let him lead. Their eyes did not stop having a conversation until hers rolled up so deep she could no longer open them.

And as her personal favorite type as herself, he was sexual and sensual in ways people were embarrassed to be. They had no taboos. No right or wrong places to touch or kiss. He was going about her body as a rare orgasms collector. For the first time in years, he was so good that she started to doubt her own level of good because his good seemed a level skiller than hers. He noticed her mind came back to her from far away planets he sent it to, and he stopped to allow her to show him what her month could do. It took her a second to regain her self-confidence back on top where it belonged. "Soooo gooood," with an European accent, sounded better than many winning awards she received for her involvement in different competitions in the past.

And after they both seemed more than happy mentally and emotionally satisfied from finally making this collision of two individuals happen, he laid on top of her and entered her body the most natural usual way, like loving each other people have sex, but what she felt was far from anything usual. He stretched her body to almost breaking point with every stroke, taking her from the highest heights to the deepest depths. Many times, she honestly said, she had the best sex in her life. She never lied. She had many best sexes in her life with different partners in different ways. And this time was not an exception. It was another best sex of it's own in it's own one-of-a-kind category.

What happened or not happened after is irrelevant. You might never hear her speak of him ever again, or you just keep watching the TV show.

CHAPTER 27

Real Fifty Shades

*"Yes, she could try to fill as loving Ana Steele to save a life,
but in this story, Ana was older and much more experienced
to know there are about four billion men on this planet and
someone else could provide her the love she wanted
in a less painful way"*

Iconic Fifty Shades books and movie series have affected all layers of the adult world. Everyone took something for themselves from the story. Some understood it, and some ultimately did not. Women adored it. Men hated it and made fun of it, comparing themselves and their skills to red room skills Christian Grey possessed. She herself was inspired by the made-up story of love and affection, turning a lost sadist into an exemplary man of honor.

Every tenth profile on Seeking Arrangement was named using fragments of Fifty Shades. Endless "Better Than Grey," "Fifty Shades of Dallas," "Darker than Fifty Shades," and "I will show you Fifty Shades," and they went on and on. Others often described themselves very close to Christian Grey's character portrayed in or out of his red room. And absolutely everyone using Grey's reference stated they were clearly better than Christian Grey himself if he was real.

She had never met anyone coming even close to Christian Grey's character. Some were skilled lovers with financial empires but with bad looks. Others were handsome, generous to a fault, and completely useless in bed. Occasionally she ran into the combination of good looks, extreme financial fortune, and an incredible sex drive. Still, emotionally those men were little children, insecure, constantly trying to fill in the black hole inside them with an idea of a life they owned but did not really enjoy.

There was this extremely popular profile on Seeking. The profile had a Diamond status, and it had a background-verified badge. The profile was always on the first page when you opened an app or a website. He was a gorgeous, tall, middle eastern looking man with a beautiful athletic body. Multiple women surrounded him in his pictures, private jets, all smiles, and fun. Over a hundred million worth mark did not hurt his profile at all. And no, he was not Dan Bilzerian. This guy looked like a model, and he was hot and sexy in a natural-born way. He was the type any woman with any preferences would turn their head after. He looked like a Persian king from a romantic novel all girls like to read about. A modern-day-looking Viking type. Just his good looks raised questions.

There was no doubt his profile was slammed with messages from every female on Seeking. She sent him a message too. She did not intend to get a response. She simply inputted her admiration for his existence on this planet because he definitely stood out in the crowd. She did not remember what she wrote, but it was something simple, like "Definitely one of a kind." And a few weeks after, he responded. He also found her profile very special, and they had to meet. And they met the same day, a few hours after she finished work, and drove across town to what must be the only place still open late in his area on a weeknight.

She arrived first, and she took a table for two outside, overlooking the driveway of the lounge. She opened his Seeking profile again and started to look closely, trying to get a better picture of the character of the perfect-looking guy she was meeting. The women he was surrounded by in his pictures were not models or anything beautiful at all. Regular-looking females, judging by the style of clothes and accessories, were from small regular American towns in a lesser populated state. And this was interesting because he could have chosen a more interesting company of women as an entourage. But he did not.

He arrived in a simple American-made car every middle-class family like to own. He was dressed in a simple way, with nothing giving out an idea of his financial fortune. He was very handsome. And it came to her. He was not local. And it was very refreshing for a change. A beautiful, smart, successful guy who was not stocked up or hung up on the idea of showing off!

He sat down on a high chair beside her, and time flew by. They talked and talked like two people who have known each other all their lives. He shared his life story, he shared where he stands right now, and he shared what his dreams are all about. They spoke about his work. She looked at her watch; it was almost midnight, and she remembered why they were there. It was time to get to the point. So, she asked him why he was single and looking for an arrangement. He seemed like a dream come true, a perfect man for any woman. What did she miss?

He was looking at her. They were silent for a good minute. And he said, "Maybe we can talk about it another time, I am enjoying your company, and I don't want you to misunderstand me." Odd if not say much. She touched his leg with her knee under the table to give him the idea she wanted to continue this conversation. He pulled his leg away. Another odd.

She looked down at the table for a few seconds in silence and looked at him again, "I don't think I will see you again if you refuse to discuss a possible arrangement we both arrived here to seek." He took a deep breath and pulled out his smartphone.

He opened his Seeking page, which was lit up in red notifications. She had not seen anything like this yet. With over eight thousand unanswered messages, he was favored by over fourteen thousand female profiles. What he was trying to say was unclear, but she could not stop thinking about how did he find her in this mess. Odd and confusing. She looked at him again, and he clearly understood it was time for him to explain himself.

He talked, and she listened without interfering. The more he spoke, the colder she felt.

His preferences in the relationship between him and his chosen one were unusual, to say nothing. He truly enjoyed overpowering, humiliating, and disrespecting the one he chose to love. And finally, a real-life character came to light who definitely overshone fantastic sadist Christian Grey.

After good fifteen minutes of explanatory details, he originally chose not to scare her with on the first date, she got up, thanked him for tea, and was ready to leave. No, she did not stop liking, respecting, or admiring him as a person. She was no longer interested in him as a man for herself. He had nothing she was looking for. Yes, she could try to fill as loving Ana Steele to save a life, but in this story, Ana was older and much more experienced to know there are about four billion men on this planet, and someone else could provide her with the love she wanted in a less painful way.

He stood up from his chair and gently put both of her arms tight behind her back. He was holding her tight against his body and whispering in her ear how much she would like him fucking her hard with his big dick, with her being all tied up and not being able to move and refuse him. Her breathing changed, and he smiled. Yes, she was aroused. She was aroused physically. Any man or woman could get her to that point. But here, him in particular, mentally, he was not able to breach her walls. He did not have it in him. And she felt sorry for him.

She hugged him goodbye. All his body tensed up. He did not like it, he did not want to be touched. She started to walk away toward her car.

"Anything you want, come tomorrow to my house!" he shouted to her, disappearing from his view, but she was already gone.

CHAPTER 28

Good Guys

"He did not know what love is and for that reason he could not gift it to those who needed it the most"

Good guys. Good guys are mostly married, separated, or newly divorced. They are the ones who know how to be partners. They have patience, they are gentle, and they care. Good guys are perfect for any woman who is ready to settle down. Settle down not necessarily for love but for stability and security.

Newly divorced men do still remember the warm, comforting feeling of having a family. They did not yet cross over to at first exciting and wild single-life side, turning into sadness and despair a few years later. Once one had a family, the greatest gift of all, one would always want to have one again, for better reasons and with more right for you person.

She used to think she was looking for strictly a good guy like this until and this dream came true.

His Seeking profile was great. Forty-nine (!) years old, newly divorced man, three middle school children, successful auto-industry business, beautiful, organized life, intelligent, handsome, athletic, and funny. Since she responded to his first message, their communication flowed pleasantly and easily. There was something extremely warm coming from him, this feeling was luring her in, she had the same warmth inside her, and she knew that rare and wonderful feeling well.

They had planned to meet and go out to dinner. He lived an hour away. Getting to him on a weekday after work was already an adventure. One hour in a car could turn into two at any highway exit. Their state was famous for bad drivers, and if it were raining, everyone would just pull by the sides of the highway and wait. Almost three million people population in her city, and barely anyone knew how to drive.

She parked in a beautiful driveway of a private golf community. Peacocks gracefully walked around everywhere as far as you could see. She got out of her car and saw him for the first time. He was standing at the entrance to the residential building dressed up in a tight white button-down shirt and skinny jeans. He looked different in his pictures online. There, he was a good-looking classy American guy. Here in person, he could quickly join Jonas Brothers, and no one would notice an extra edition. She was attracted to him instantly, but why he was all dressed up like a teenager, she could not understand.

They said hi to each other, and silence never ever entered their life. He was wonderful. They gracefully interrupted each other in a hurry to share the excitement they were both feeling from the meeting. She could be perfectly herself around him, he was smart, and her funny, sharp jokes came exactly as they meant without being misunderstood hundred times. He was a breath of fresh air in many weeks of searching for the one she could dissolve herself in safely.

Her high heels were floating on a pebble road leading them to a restaurant at the club. The weather was perfect for a late April night. She was very much into him as she lost all count of time and her location. If someone stopped her right now, she would have no idea where she was, and there was no way she could return to her car by herself.

At the entrance to the club, they stumbled on a group of people, and her fairy tale just stopped. Those people were parents and other family members to a woman and mother of his children he had just recently divorced. An unpleasant coincidence, you would think. He introduced her to about ten people, and she patiently waited for a storm of bad memories and emotions to hunt him for the rest of the evening. But to her surprise, they had more similar qualities in common! His in-laws loved him, and he loved them all back.

Dinner was romantic and delightful. He was a great conversationalist with an exciting outlook on everything. As herself, he could read between the lines, and he did it faster and better than her, to say the least. His energy level and brain power were more than enough to run for a senate and more, but he chose to stay in a family business. That might have been the original bad idea whete he made a wrong turn many years ago. He was an obvious genius stuck in ordinary life, he was trying to fit into all his life. He was failing at it, but he did not know it yet himself.

Every minute, every life story, he looked more and more attractive to her, she was wondering where the devil was hiding here, but tonight she did not find it. Her evening was a real-life fairy tale, she could not get enough of her date, and the date felt exactly the same.

A couple of hours later, they magically made it back to his residence same mysterious way she could not trace again. She was happy for the first time in weeks. Nothing else mattered. Not just started to sprinkle rain, not the bottoms of her heels getting stuck on a pebble road.

He stopped by her car and asked if she wanted to meet his dog upstairs. She nodded, and even if they kept talking after that, it was all a blur. Because he went above and beyond to make her feel majestic things the moment they stepped inside his apartment.

The height of his bed was perfect for a triathlon of feelings and emotions he walked her thru that late April evening. He was not holding back anything. He excelled at licking and sucking, twisting and turning, gently slow to powerful hard, among other very nice enjoyable things.

And it lasted. It was perfectly wonderful until she realized he did not know what love was. He was following the scenario of his first marriage. Here he was, failing for the same reason once again. It had to look good for the world. A beautiful café with no taste. He was the perfect provider, caretaker, friend, partner, father, and many other characters but one thing. He did not know what love was, so he could not gift it to those who needed it the most.

CHAPTER 29

Wonder People

"Perhaps dinner, maybe lunch. Possibly just a tea at the bar.
Or maybe she just took an elevator upstairs
straight into his room"

Wonder people. You know of them, but you know nothing about them. They change the lives of many people doing their regular jobs. They are the core of industries and businesses. We often see them on TV, eating lunch by themselves at restaurants in different capitals of the world. We admire the fantastic athletic shape they are in and fashion forward business attire they wear. They are like a front page of a Forbes Magazine, and you can get a glimpse of them, but never the whole picture. And there is a reason for it. And the reason is there is nothing past the cover page.

Looking back, she did not remember any of the details or specifics of how exactly they met thru Seeking arrangement. He was the fourth lucky man she went on a date with within the first three or four months of her SA journey. It was the last few months of the year. It might have been one of the great restaurants in one of the best hotels in the city. Perhaps dinner, maybe lunch. Possibly just a tea at the bar. Or maybe she just took an elevator upstairs straight into his room.

He was tall and handsome. Jet black wavy hair. Brown eyes. Big puffy lips. And a genuine but suppressed smile. If she did not know he was a part of one of the best active investment management companies, he could play a role of a politician very well. He kept two residences in major cities in a county, where his things lived, while he was living in hotels in between the flights. There was no family of his own, kids, pets, or friends in his past.

She did not remember if they even talked on their first date. She remembered the eye contact neither of them wanted to brake for the duration of that first hour, but she did not remember talking to him. She used to be like that in her early twenties. She did not know how to talk to people, so she just listened. This time, it was not like that, as she became a fantastic conversationalist over the last ten years. He had a great voice, and he sounded incredible in all the financial interviews she regularly watched him give on the news.

Maybe he wondered about her, and he was fighting his desire to connect deeper with her. Maybe, like everyone else she met, he felt like she was like no one he had ever met. Perhaps he was wondering what she was wondering about looking at him. And she was wondering how it was possible for him from successfully working for Disney to jump into a completely different profession and instantly succeed at it.

For their second date, he freed up all the second part of his day for her. It was obvious he wanted more, he wanted, but he could not. As soon as their wild sex race was over, he looked at her, and again, he could not say a word. She counted four empty condom wrappers on the nightstand and smiled. To make it easier for him, she left. She was not facilitating the conversation, and she knew he needed a chance to make a change on his own. She hoped he would because, as with anyone else, she entered his life to improve it, and sooner or later, that would happen. It always does.

He was someone very beautiful on the inside, but he was not sharing that person with anyone. And suddenly and unexpectedly, their third date started with a dinner at a wonderful restaurant with a twelve-course tasting menu. It was looking a lot like two to three hours of looking at each other in silence. All she hoped was that he would not leave halfway thru dinner, but that did not happen either. He let her in, and he let her into his world and his thoughts. He let her into his memories and feelings about the world and people. His personal world was very small and private. He was dedicated to his work, he was over forty years old, and the majority of it was responsibly spent on caring for the financial stability and security of others. He was the type of man who would make a fantastic husband and a father if he only let some good woman in. It was not her. She was here for a particular amount of time, and she was looking to enrich her already perfect life with emotions not many knew existed. But she wished for him to maybe one day get out of his shell and do something normal, like having a family of his own.

Years went by, and those two became closer, and she hoped she did change his life for the better. She hoped he would work a little less and live a little more. She loved herself, and she was able to show everyone she cared for how to get there. He never got a real girlfriend, and he is still not married. But he did something wonderful for himself, in secret.

Next time you are at a concert at your neighborhood theatre or concert hall, look around and listen. One of the singers will stand out significantly. He will look like a Wall Street guy, but he will sing his heart out like Michael Crawford in Phantom of the Opera.

CHAPTER 30

Love and Madness

"They can't possibly just relax and enjoy it, they want to break this feeling down to try to understand it and control it, for the one reason – to keep it forever, not realizing that not the feeling they need to keep and cherish, but the woman who made them feel that way"

Love and madness. There are many different feelings and sensations we people call love. Love comes to us and takes over, and at some point, we start to notice it. Some fall in love at first sight. Some - years after. The madness we create ourselves by being unable to process this wonderful feeling of love. Not because we don't want to, but because we want to very much, and we just don't know how to go about it. All of this is very unfortunate because we must go into the relationship to learn how to love, care and respect each other. But somehow, we crash and brake the one we desire the most instead.

She had been in love multiple times in her life. The more mature and more educated she became – the stronger and

more powerful her love stories were. The deeper she dived in
– the harder it was to breathe. Those intense couple of months
made her feel alive more than anything else she ever did. Every
single time. She was happy, but it was unhealthy. Both parties always were aware that it was not how normal happiness
felt. Maybe all of them were just not the happy kind. Suffering
from childhood issues all their lives, they never learned how to
let themselves be loved. Taken advantage of – yes, loved – no.
Not yet.

She attracted the same mad kind as her. Men she loved
were fearless, smart, and rebellious. All of them always knew
what exactly they wanted, and they all enjoyed great lives that
they built themselves from scratch…. "Started from the bottom, and now we are here." For some of them, she was the
first woman they ever loved. Imagine a fifty to sixty years old
successful man who just fell in love for the first time in their
full of experiences life. They can't possibly just relax and enjoy
it. They want to break this feeling down to try to understand
it and control it, for one reason – to keep it forever, not realizing that not the feeling they need to keep and cherish but the
woman who made them feel that way.

She expected generosity on all fronts, from daily affection
to full financial support. Men desired full disclosure and loy-
alty. She battled her desire to be a little girl, and they battled
their desire to control her. She spent hundreds of hours in
therapy to learn how to admit to herself her greatness and be
a partner, not a daughter, in a relationship. Men always dealt
with the emotional issues of starting their life over again. They
all were on a path to transformation into greater, happier ver-
sions of themselves. One must be in pain to restructure their
mind. Maybe this excruciating pain of wanting to be together
but not knowing how to – was the engine of their transfor-
mations. She really hoped so. She could not stop wondering
why two smart mature people could not figure out how to be

together when they wanted to. Sad memories of her last love were hunting her weekly. Pain from her current fall into love was physically destroying her body.

The first time she saw his photos in his Seeking profile, she had a strong feeling they already knew each other. Almost twice her age, very good-looking and in shape, a decent number of millions worth, and separated.

She patiently sat in the lobby of the building he claimed he lived in and waited. She wondered why he was living here. It was a beautiful brand-new condominium, but the location… no one mature in their right mind would live here. The quality of the people she was surrounded by was on a scale of three out of ten. And suddenly, he walked towards her. He was beautiful. Everything was beautiful about him. Eyes with another different universe in them. Glowing moist skin. Lean athletic body. He had the same energy she had. That is what she was feeling all along. They were the same kind.

Later that same night, she already knew she was in love. She was not in a rush for anything except to see him again and again. She knew what she was feeling and how rare that feeling was to find. She hoped it would last forever, but she refused to think about anything but what and how she felt in the present time having him by her side, loving him with all her existence. Just simply unconditionally loving him.

The more time they shared, the more he needed to scale the level of her love. He had no boundaries and no respect for her privacy. Genuinely appreciating her affection, he always pointed out it could have been larger or deeper. He and time together was the only thing she thought about, but he thought she did not think of him enough. Many times a day, he mentioned she thinks only of herself, and who would think of him? He was joking; every hurtful sentence coming out of his mouth at her was a joke, but it did not feel like it. It felt like a stub in a heart with a knife. And he was looking her right in the eyes while doing that.

Their arrangement stage was over, and their relationship status was not created yet. They hanged in a limbo of uncertainty. She was always there to support him. She had an honest selfish desire to help him overcome all his mental tortures, so he finishes with his inner problems and starts to be happy with her in real life. She was convinced she had enough knowledge to guide him in the right direction to reinvent himself as a person, and she hoped her love would light the way for him to see her. To truly see her. He kept telling his close friends that he thought she was partially blind or death to want to be with him, but what he was not realizing – he was describing himself.

He always held her hand while walking on the street and kissed her repeatedly, and it did not matter if they were in public or alone. The whole world seemed unreal when they were together. With time he became happier and more confident about going about all the changes in his life. At the end of their happiest days, he would text her he couldn't see her anymore because she was not right for him. She knew he was not serious, but she could not stop crying for days. The hurt was not coming from him, he acted like a two-year-old toddler eighty percent of the time. The pain came from not knowing what else to do to help him to grow up emotionally.

Sex and lovemaking were thru the roof. Never in her life had she felt so fully connected to anyone. Their bodies fit into each other like they were continuous parts of one another. It was never bad, not enough, or uncomfortable, and it was perfect every single time. He could not get himself off her. It was undecided who wanted each other more. In the most intimate moments, she would open her eyes to see his eyes stare deep into hers, and she knew deep inside he felt he should never let her go, but he was a numbers guy, and feeling things were not in his nature. He was an expert in most precious diamonds, shiny stones, fascinating the entire world, was a regular thing to him. If people could be diamonds, she would have been a rare one-of-a-kind yellow diamond, and he still would not care. Could that be because he had so many diamonds he was focused on quantity, not quality?

It was a beautiful Saturday they had spent together, maybe the best Saturday they ever had, and as on all happiest days, he needed to add something little extra of just miserable himself. She was wearing one of his favorite t-shirts over her naked body, and they cuddled on a white leather couch in his living room, looking at the sunset. The sky was bright pink, they lived in a city with the most beautiful sunsets. It was bothering him that she still had not deleted her Seeking profile, it was bothering him she had friendly lunches with her ex-boyfriend every week, it was bothering him she played golf with men they knew in common, and it was bothering him she had enough interesting men in her life to write a book about it.

Her iPhone fell on the white carpet, and when she picked it up, another long black hair was attached to it. She was blond. His daughter and his ex-wife were not brunettes. And she said, "I can recommend your maid some good hair products to stop losing so much hair." He felt very giving that evening, much more letting out than she ever expected. He was talking, she was listening and not breating. While seeing her, he had other arrangements, hookups, and relationships with multiple women. He was still legally married to his ex-wife, and he was not going to divorce her.

And she realized, indeed, she was partially blind and death.

She was driving home and crying. She was crushed and broken. Somehow, she was ok with that. But she did not know what to do with feelings she had for him. She could turn hurt into anger and anger into energy to work more and to make even more money, but no money in the world made her feel as happy as he did.

And as on any great day they spend together, the text message came, "I love being with you, your energy, your wisdom. This breaks me – but I can't see you anymore."

CHAPTER 31

Secret Traditional Ordinary

*"Looking at him she wished for more, but more never had
a place in an arrangement relationship"*

You would think men search for arrangements to spice up
their ordinary married lives or long-term relationships, or
maybe fill in the occasional blanks with romance or sex, if they
are super busy with work, possibly someone single to avoid
any responsibilities of traditional relationships or emotional
attachment.

His Seeking profile did not fit the criteria she preferred.
He was just a few years older than her but was very physically attractive. He was not a multimillionaire with exciting
life experiences, what could produce the lock of subjects to
talk about if they wanted to speak. But something so calm and
steady was in an overall feeling about his profile. She wanted

to feel that calm in person. So, she decided to throw her usual upfront approach, directly in his face, hoping he would feel intimidated by the arrangement terms she demanded, that she could tell herself ordinary men are not her thing again. But he was up to anything to get a chance to get to know her.

He had only one free day a week to do his all-non-work-related activities. Soon few hours of that day became the normality she did seek in her life. Tuesdays became little holidays. He would always arrive later than she expected, and he never stayed long enough for her, even remotely, to feel they were in some sort of relationship. She wondered why his Tuesdays started with gym, barber, and a few other things he did and not with her. He wanted to be with her in a way she did not understand. He was very well emotionally put together and calm, always calm. He rarely smiled or expressed any emotions at all. He was just there with her in the same room, living her life, and for the most part, he was listening to everything she had to share with him that day. He never started a conversation himself, he never started anything himself, but he would always stop her if she wanted to feel something he was not sharing.

He was tall with a great posture, cut short dark hair, and, rare for their state location, white skin. He must have worked out every single day, his body could put to shame any twenty years old young man. You could see the definition of his abs through the casual t-shirts he always wore. He had the class in him, the same class every American man had sixty years ago, the manners, the attitude. He was charming to be around because he was not letting her anywhere closer than that.

Their first three hours date, he spent sitting at her dining table eating her homecooked breakfast and listening to her stories. She lost count of how many teas they had that day. He was not giving out any emotions, she did not know if he was into her at all, but he was not leaving. Until he got up, thanked her, and left. She did not know what to think. It was unusual.

Some Tuesdays after he ate, he kissed her on the lips before he left, other Tuesdays, she tried to get him into bed, and occasionally, she succeeded. Fully dressed under covers, he hugged and kissed her until she wanted to do the same. It never happened, she could feel and see he was fully aroused and hard for her, but she was not allowed even to touch him. It was getting frustrating.

Officially he lived alone with his little daughter, and he was not married or in a relationship with anyone. Unofficially she did not understand who he was holding himself back for.

Some days he shared his life stories, his teenage memories. He was genuine, pleasant, and great. He could socialize with others, lead at work, be in relationships and marriages, and raise happy kids. He cared for his body, ate extremely healthily, and did a good job being himself.

She did not understand the platonic aspect of their arrangement, but she respected it. After all, not once he intentionally made her feel unwanted or undesired. Looking at him, she wished for more, but more never had a place in an arranged relationship.

CHAPTER 32

Wanting Change

"She knew a lot of married couples and not one who were perfectly honest with one another"

That Friday morning, she woke up wanting changes. She wanted new people in her life. She changed over the last few months, and there were things she was no longer willing to tolerate in herself and others. These changes came quickly, she was at ease with herself, and she wanted someone easy to have an arrangement where she could be herself at all times and be loved just as she was. She did not want to try to seem calmer, sexier, simple, or whatever else she used to think she must become. She was finally happy with herself as she was. She always smiled and laughed, spreading the love around her, inspiring people to finally start living their lives, speaking up her opinion on everything, and saying "no" to whatever felt like "no" to her. She was happy and knew what she wanted and where to get it fast.

Exiting early morning reformer Pilates class, she turned the ringer of her iPhone on and logged in to Seeking Arrangement. Seventeen new messages since she checked last night. She had time to respond to the first four until one of them was online, and the chat became instant.

Fifty-seven years old married businessman in an open marriage, two grown children, his fleet of planes, speed boats, houses in multiple states, fantastic surfer body, and a genuinely welcoming smile. He loved good food, traveling, and was picky about who he was sharing his time with. A rare kind of American born. Self-educated, self-made, and self-sufficient. He was perfect. And that was the part where she usually would get suspicious. But this morning, she decided to believe people like him existed, good in and out, with pure intentions to simply love the company of another without any agenda behind it.

The communication by text flowed easily. He agreed to everything she suggested and instantly adjusted to the new plan once what she wanted was not possible that lunchtime. Nothing could stand in her way of enjoying her day and her possible easy new arrangement.

This time she did not wear a dress, she did not try to tame her hair, and Jimmy Choo was left behind on a high heels shelf. Ruffle mini skirt barely covered her back, showing off her perfectly toned legs. Long sleeve crop top left her tight stomach open for the public to enjoy. Smiling, she exited her car and walked her Havaianas flip-flops to a family-owned Italian restaurant on the corner of the block. He was already sitting at a table outside in a ninety degrees summer heat. She kissed him on the cheek and landed in a chair across the table from him. She enthusiastically smiled and took her sunglasses off.

He adored her from the moment she arrived till the end of the next two and a half hours of their lunch.

To him, she was the most intelligent, exciting, and simply the most gorgeous woman he had ever met.

To her, she was just herself, and she greatly appreciated he was able to "see the real her." She was having a good time and was okay if this lunch was the only time they shared. He looked at her the way people look at the original Mona Lisa in the Louvre. He loved what he was looking at, but she was unsure if he was brave enough to take a step further. Men are afraid of women like her. She was impossible to control and knew more about any subject than most. She did not want to be challenged; she wanted to be loved. Not many men could do that, and she was unsure if he wanted to try. She thanked him for lunch, and he said, "I can't wait to do it again! Tuesday night?"

She could not do Tuesday night. She could do Friday evening, exactly a week from today. So, it was decided. They parted ways happily. This day that man turned out exactly as she wished for until he texted her the same evening and asked to move the next date to late tomorrow morning because he could not wait a moment longer to see her again.

The next day she got up thinking how nice was the moment her hand touched his chest when they were saying goodbye after lunch yesterday. It felt familiar. The feeling was warm and welcoming. She desired him. It did not drive her crazy, and it gave her comfort. She wanted to have more of that feeling. Felling of normality, and she already hoped that it would last. She needed to recharge and ground herself. And he seemed like a perfect man for a job.

Today she desired to be different for him. She wore a beautiful crochet white dress and her favorite pair of beige lacy Jimmy Choo heels. The highway going north was empty, and the drive, which usually would take her an hour, took barely half an hour.

He picked a beautiful lunch spot on the water overlooking large boats. They were no longer in a big city, and she dramatically stood out in a crowd of mediocre-looking women. He mentioned his house is literary around the corner. She knew his wife was home with him yesterday and, most likely, today. He said they live in an open marriage. In the past, everyone she met stated they had an open marriage like that, were lying and hiding their infidelity from their wives. She knew a lot of married couples and not one who was perfectly honest with one another. But the fact that he was not worried about them being seen together at lunch gave her hope. Maybe this particular time, his marriage was the type she never experienced in the past before.

The food was healthy and as fantastic as in all Hillstone group restaurants. She was finishing up her salad and thinking about where he planned to take her after lunch.

After the check was paid and they found their cars outside, he asked her to follow him to his house. She was confused. The last thing she needed right now was any drama or possible misunderstanding. Her memory was impeccable, no wife was in the discussed arrangement. And now, all of a sudden, he was taking her home. Home where he lived with his wife.

He was watching her, looking all confused, she remained calm, but she no longer smiled. He figured if he did not say something immediately, this romantic afternoon could fast downhill from wonderful lunch to nothing.

"She is not home. She is visiting her mother in a town over this afternoon," he said, "And she knows you are coming over, and it is okay," – he continued. She nodded and drove behind his car, following him to his house.

Nothing dishonest was happening. All parties were in on making this arrangement work. Nothing was wrong. He was charming, pleasant, and wonderful. She liked him very much and looked forward to seeing how much more wonderful they could feel together. But in those couple of minutes of driving, her past caught up to her.

She remembered returning home in her second marriage and finding little things her ex-husband's lovers would leave behind to state their occasional presence in their house. She believed he never took them past the guest bedroom, but the realization of someone else being in her space, her sacred, secure safe place, was deeply painful, if you could put it in two words. Yes, now and before, she had affairs and arrangements with married men, but it was all by the rules that not one wife would ever find out. The last thing she wanted to do on Earth was to cause any kind of pain to anyone.

His house looked like a model-home realtor would set it up with nice furniture to sell quickly. Four huge luggage were placed by the front door. She pointed out that this place looked straight from the market, and he told her he had moved into the house yesterday.

Every time she changed the place of living, she made it at least a month-long transition. This guy flew in from another state yesterday, met her for lunch, moved into an entirely brand-new house later that day, and dedicated half a day to her again a few hours later, the next day! Who does that?! She was starting to feel amused by the whole thing. Jokes aside, looking at him now, she realized how important she had become to him. She calmed down. She was feeling grateful, welcomed, and appreciated. And wanted, he wanted her very much.

Do you know what men can do in bed when they fall in love with the woman of their dreams? A complete dictionary of pleasant words. If they were not lying in the same bed where his wife slept last night, we could make two dictionaries of pleasant words, but she could not stop thinking how odd all this was to her. He seemed perfectly fine, like nothing unordinary was happening in his family bedroom.

CHAPTER 33

Wasted Time

*"Facebook has a funny way of connecting people who are not
necessarily need to be re-connected"*

Facebook has a funny way of connecting people who do
not necessarily need to be reconnected. If it was only
about childhood friends, fun school years, or relatives, but
nowadays, in a way many of us regular users don't understand,
we are reconnecting with people we gladly left in the past. He
Facebook-friended her a few years after that strange evening they
spent together. She sincerely believed one could get something
good or learn something new from anyone, especially someone
like him. But that evening, he managed to waste over five hours
of her life and not provide anything in return. An evident
disappointment she wished not to remember.

It was at the beginning of her Seeking Arrangement journey. She was excited, and she had no expectations. She had no
rules, no limitations. She was welcoming and pleasant, and all
she wanted in return for her company was a good time.

Another forty-nine years old handsome man. Tall, athletic doctor. He showed his beautiful smile in numerous pictures with his A-list celebrity clients: at sporting events, art show-cases, and high-end parties. Work photos from his practice were filled with models looking women. He was a member of Seeking years before, he knew the rules of the game, and she was confident he knew what he was doing when he wanted to meet her.

They picked an evening for dinner, and she drove forty-five minutes north a few days later. She was never fond of the location she was going; her vibe was higher frequency than anyone in that area had. But he seemed very energetic, having hobbies like clubbing at his age. So, she took a chance.

The restaurant he picked was brand new, modern tapas-style cuisine: sushi, raw fish tacos, ceviche, all the things she loved. The selection of hot green teas won her over completely. He arrived right on time, and the chemistry between them was obvious. He looked like the boy she loved in high school; he gave out the same comforting, familiar feeling. Maybe because he was a doctor, but not all doctors had the ability to get in a friendly zone so fast. He seemed like an extremely pleasant man to be around. He seemed.

The odd thing was he started the conversation talking about himself only. During the two-and-a-half-hour dinner, he did not ask her anything about her and her life, not one ques-tion. She thought he must have been very lonely if he needed to pour his life struggles on her. It was not bad. It was just one-sided. She was playing a role of a listener while she wanted to connect.

His twenty years long marriage ended for no particular rea-son. He and his ex-spouse continued to work together every day. Everything and everyone seemed to be mildly happy. But then he started to talk about a girl. Someone he was passion-ate about in a fatherly-friendly, supportive and protective way.

Young girl. She listened, and she stopped smiling. He was pouring his heart out to a stranger; all she could think about was Nabokov's "Lolita."

His Seeking profile stated he wanted to meet a woman between twenty-six and forty-four years old. He was on an arranged date with a beautiful thirty-something years old woman who looked like twenty-six. They had instant chemistry. This could have been the beginning of something memorable. But he chose to tell this beautiful young woman everything he had on his mind and heart about his Lolita.

He met his Lolita at a party and was unsure how old she was. She was not local and lived either in her car or at anyone else's place she could spend the night. Gorgeous skinny blond Lolita was so helpless, he could not let it be as it was. He had an instant need to save her and protect her. He hired her to do social media work for his practice and helped her rent an apartment with her girlfriend. He took her with him everywhere he could. She was grateful to have a new father figure. He felt needed and fulfilled. But it seemed like he needed something she was not seeing in him. He was a father, but deep inside, a father wanted to be seen as the man she desired. She did not desire him. She desired young men around him.

He looked at his phone every fifteen minutes, and she enjoyed probably the eighth plate of food they ordered. The food was good. It might have been the only good thing that evening. She wondered if she was mistaken and if he did care about the girl in a usual human way. She asked if he was waiting for an important call on his cell phone. He responded with an explanation. His Lolita was at a dinner with his good-looking young friend right now. Lolita was a drinker, and he was worried she might have needed his help. That's so. She started to feel annoyed. No, this was not jealousy. This poor guy was in love and might not have even realized it. And here he was, wasting her precious evening. She leaned across the table towards him and looked him straight in the eyes to see if there was some chance he was under some magic spell. He smiled, touched her cheek, and asked, "Should we get out of here?".

She nodded. She was curious about what he was in the mood to do next.

His penthouse was small and cozy. They walked straight into the bedroom, and her mood started to pick up again. He did not say a word about Lolita since they left the restaurant. He held her hand, and he opened doors for her. He was relaxed and seemed to be having a good time. She did not know what to make of him, all she hoped for at that moment was hot sex, and she was hoping it would happen sooner than later.

He sat her down in a lovely soft chair across his bed, grabbed his guitar from the corner of his bed, and started playing. At first, it seemed romantic. She had never been a big fan of guitar play, especially at eleven in the evening after a long work day and a strange dinner conversation. He had a conversation, she just listened.

Good forty minutes after, she lost her patience. Who in the world wants to hear ten or more songs tonight? His talented doctor hands were likely capable of much more than just a guitar play. She got up from the chair and slowly took her dress off while making the distance to reach him. She grabbed his guitar and gently put it down on the floor. She was not risking to trigger any non-sex-related reaction in him. Getting on top of him and starting to kiss was finally the first thing she enjoyed today, except for the food they ate. Going for his zipper, all she hoped was to feel him hard. If he was hard, they were game. And he was; all his beautiful manhood was on the same level of excitement as her.

Happy, she went down and started sucking him as passionately as she felt towards this man the minute he walked into the restaurant hours before. And ten seconds after, he came. She looked up at him with a question in her eyes. He looked like nothing happened that he did not plan on. He looked happy. She was getting mad. She asked him if he would get hard again after a little break, but he responded, "Not tonight, for sure."

She picked up her dress from the floor and started to walk downstairs to leave. He said something to her, but she did not hear him anymore. She never wanted to hear from him ever again. Never. What a waste of time.

CHAPTER 34

Mission Impossible

"He was not just recently lost, he was lost all his life"

There are times in single life when everyone you love around you is in a relationship. New relationships most likely won't last because around you are the same type of exceptional people as you are. Freedom lovers, good-doers, and finally, emotionally stable self-loving people. The type can no longer be controlled, manipulated, or limited by anything or anyone. The kind that does not settle for anything less than unconditional, honest love. And that is the reason it could never last in the town they are all living in. Too many wealthy men, too many gorgeous women. But once in a while, we try again and again.

That day all three of her last loves were unavailable to maintain her friendship. Their new girlfriends were jealous of her and the place she took in every one of those men's minds and hearts. She hoped to make each of those men The One at different years of her life. When it did not happen, after months of painful separations, they reconnected as friends, because once you truly love someone, you can no longer let them go. They became friends, not many can understand friendship like that, but she could, and she cherished it while she had it. On this particular day, friends she loved had to stop their occasional lunches and dinners not to piss off their new girlfriends' lack of confidence and self-esteem.

It was not that she had nothing else to do. She was busy with school and work, had arrangements, and traveled. But not having the people you love around you was a dramatic difference. She was sad. She knew it was all temporary. And the idea came to her to do something normal by society's standards. Her exes' new relationship statuses inspired her to go on an absolutely normal date. She did not like normal, but she had the energy and desire to try this subject again.

To be absolutely honest, it did not start like this. This chapter started a year ago and has nothing to do with the events she experienced earlier today, finding out she is entirely cast away by the ones she loved the most. This news was hurtful and took her off track of the real story.

A year ago, she was trying to give herself something she was not sure she needed, but the idea of a normal traditional relationship was on her mind, as anything– she had to make it her reality. And she did. Fast and effective.

Out of all available meeting men of her caliber sites, she chose Millionaire Match. She created an absolutely honest encyclopedia-like profile with lots of information, real-life pictures, and full disclosure of what kind of man she was looking for. This type of openness was supposed to eliminate everyone who was not Him. She was proud of how far she had come in being truthful about herself. She saved her perfect profile and exited the website for a week.

She was excited and optimistic. She thought over a dating plan on how she will make time for this new person in her life for this possible new relationship she is about to have. She truly believed her actions would change possibly all of her life in a new direction she always wanted. The idea of finding The One seemed like minutes away from happening.

Over seven days, seventy-eight millionaires applied for a position to date her. It took her over three and a half hours to look at their profiles and read from top to bottom all the information these men provided about themselves.

Only one fits the profile. He was the first to write her. It seemed unreal that she chose the one who saw her first out of seventy-eighth, but it was real. Maybe the universe finally gifted her something she wanted easily and with no surprises. Maybe she finally deserved her own happiness.

She responded to his message, and he responded instantly.

She did not know how to explain all of this, but this guy was turning out to be exactly what she had been looking for all these years. He was from out of town but was moving into her neighborhood in three weeks. Men from out of town had a different feel for beautiful women, and they wanted just one, not realizing how many they could really have in her town. If this worked out, they both will live in her favorite place on Earth. Possibly together.

They exchanged phone numbers and picked a time to meet for coffee the same day later.

She arrived ten minutes earlier, as always. He was twenty minutes late, but he texted and called to give her a heads-up. It was a nasty rainy day, and the streets started to flood. He owned a warehouse full of exotic sports cars, and non-of them was suitable for that day's nasty weather.

He walked into a coffee shop full of energy and landed himself right next to her placing his hand on her thigh. She thought it was an offensive baller move for a first impression, but she liked it. Seeing someone still have the balls to possess a woman like that was fun. It was even funnier to find out "to bowl" is what he did to create his fortune. During those two and a half hours they spent talking over a few cups of coffee, he ended up having all balls in his court.

He was intelligent, funny, and athletic. He knew how to adjust to different situations fast. He was a walking powerhouse of all qualities she liked in a man. Modern days James Bond. And he was free. But are we ever free, are we ever fully moved on after the last relationship we lost? Are we? She felt like she was, and he talked like he was as well.

He kissed her on the mouth when she was living, passionately and in the most destructive way ever. Huh.

She was walking to her car, fantasizing about what they would do on their next date. It was a magical feeling of almost getting everything you ever wanted finally handed to you.

The next day she saw him passing by the restaurant in the same mall they were having coffee a day earlier. She wondered why he did not call or text her if he was right next to her house. He did not see her that second day at the mall. And she decided not to text first.

He did not text or call her for the next eight months. She no longer took his persona seriously, but she still was interested. After all, he was a modern-life James Bond, and who could say no to that guy?

Eight months after their first coffee date, he joined her for lunch, and they decided to spend the next few hours together. That day he somehow already knew who she was. He repeatedly said everyone he knew had to say good things about her. So, he knew people who knew her. Or he knew people who thought they knew her. Because no one really knew who she really was and how she lived.

That day he was driving his favorite car and wearing his favorite watch. That day he did not fit in this fancy neighborhood, they were driving in. He was not showing off his planes or his other toys. That day he was himself, and he wanted her to see him like that. And she loved what she saw.

They were on the way to see his latest purchase—a gorgeous yacht made of black glass. Out of hundreds of boats, she would choose the same one. What are the odds? I guess they had the same taste in things.

The next stop was his brand-new apartment in the newest building on the beach, two minutes away from her house. She did not plan to sleep with him that day. This had to be more or less a normal escalation of the normal dating experience she was aiming for here. She was curious to see if, inside his home, everything was up to her liking, as everything else she had experienced of him so far.

And she could no longer speak when he opened his apartment door. It was not possible. Everything in his apartment had a reflection of her taste and preferences. Couches, tables, lamps, colors, and textures. The golden bookcase in the middle of his living room made her freeze. Thousands of her favorite books are all in one place. After that, she no longer considered him a coincidence or an experiment. They were meant to meet, and she hoped he was meant to stay. Her mind was racing. This was the first time she met a man she could not see a possible reason to disagree on something about.

His business was shown on live TV, and that was what they were watching for the next hour and a half. Just sitting on a perfect couch, just watching TV in a perfect living room. And when the show was over, he leaned to kiss her. And she kissed him back. It was hard to stop, but she was firm on her decision to make him wait to have her. So, she leaned away and told him he won't be having sex with her today because she wanted them to try to build something special out of this together. He nodded and placed himself on the floor right in front of her. She watched his hands slowly moving her skirt up her thighs and his lips moving toward one place she desired him the most.

What he did and how he did it – was her favorite way. How a stranger could live and act so much up to her liking was mind-blowing.

When he finished kissing her, he told her he was not looking for anything serious.

Maybe he became like any other man in her town in those eight months. He realized he could have it all without any particular commitment. She was late. He was lost. Later on, she found out more. He was not just recently lost; he was lost all his life.

Three weeks after, a man with a familiar face wrote to her on Seeking arrangement.

That man was forty-nine years old, with over a million dollars in yearly income, over a hundred million net worth, two children from women he never married, and a broken bleeding heart by a young Russian woman who did not know what she wanted. A modern life James Bond. He was never free. He forever belonged to one he could not get through. Mission Impossible.

CHAPTER 35

Mixed Feelings

"It seemed he knew everything about anything,
but one thing – how to love a woman"

Mixed feelings. She met a guy; she met hundreds, maybe thousands of guys in her lifetime. This one was so different from all these interesting men she surrounded herself with. It bothered her. She could not understand what happened to him to make him so cold. He was the life of the party in every room he walked in, and he had more energy than an army of ordinary men. He was alive, and desired to do and feel things. But could he? She felt like, maybe once, for a second, she got through his walls, but that one second did not make up for hundreds of superficial hours they spent together. He refused to connect. One step closer, three steps back.

To say he did not love women was not that. Or maybe it was. It was important to him his date was happy and well taken care of. It was important to him that at that particular moment when he was with her, she was happy. But the moment they parted ways, he could not care less of anything about her. He was the gift to his women, a temporary gift, fun, engaging, and exciting! He was not interested in brightening up anyone's day if he was not present in it. He was not offering any help or assistance with anything. It seemed he knew everything about anything but one thing – how to love a woman.

At first, he opposed her idea of writing about him. And only months later, he agreed to become another story in her book.

His Seeking Arrangement profile was short and honest. He was new in town, and he was absolutely new to the game. He required steps she usually would say "no" to, but him living five minutes away from her was a beneficial factor she could not say "no" to, convenience above all. Thirty-nine years old, athletic, handsome, Asian roots, in an over two years lengthy divorce proceeding. He was obnoxiously intelligent and confident. He could expand and debate any subject better than any scientist or lawyer. He was not a public person but he was behind one of the world's biggest media companies. Decisions he made affected all of us in one way or another.

He wanted to meet her for coffee before committing to an arrangement, which unprecedently changed both of their lives. To her, this step was an unnecessary use of time. No one ever refused her. She had already picked him; how he felt about it was just a matter of minutes he spent in her presence. Maybe one day, she will invent a word woman like her could use to be described as "one perfect fit" for all kinds of great men. And until then, fifteen minutes of coffee had to take place. He was hers by the time she ordered a cup of green tea. She could not recall what they talked about for the next two and a half hours. He was consuming less than average pizza at a French restaurant they were sitting at. The look in his eyes did not hide his high interest in her persona. And she was just sitting there on a hot, humid summer night in an outdoor, liked by no one, French restaurant in her favorite mall in the middle of her favorite town. But did she like him?

Friday nights became a special time. It did not need to be confirmed; they did not need to debate what they would do and at what hour they would do it. Their time together created a new time for her and a new time for him. It felt like they have invented a new time zone just for them. He thought she liked to dine early, and she liked the fact that he thought of times of things she liked. She never understood how much he catered to her preferences, but it felt like they liked same things when they were together.

Some Friday nights, he fought her every opinion. On other Friday nights, their outlook on everything was a perfect vision of two minds colliding in one. There were no streets they did not drive on together, and almost no restaurants were left without a memory of them dining there. There were not many life stories untold. And some nights, she looked at him and wished they had similar plans for future life because the thought of not having Friday nights with him was making her whole-body freeze for reasons she did not want to understand.

He painfully bit her lip the first time they kissed. Three weeks after, she had to go to a doctor to restore hearing damage he had done to her by sticking his tongue into her ear. She might have had more pictures of bite marks and finger bruises on her body than pictures of them together. And yet he was a perfect lover to her. Like her, he could lose himself in sex completely. Time stopped existing when they were intimate, and hours passed like minutes. Sometimes she would force herself to open her eyes to see him looking at her. He never stopped looking at her, she wholly belonged to him then. He felt at home, but he was homeless.

She desired to be her man's center of the world. She desired to travel often. She desired to eat out ten times a week. She desired large diamonds. She desired to home base in her favorite city on Earth. She desired full financial support and respect for everything she was working on. He desired to create and raise motherless children. He desired to help solve problems without being obligated to do so. He desired not to be loved until he restored full control of his life and everyone in it.

But did she love him? It hurts just to think about it.

CHAPTER 36

One Beautiful Man

*"Emotional attachments and toxic relationships
even smartest of us have difficulties dealing
with experiencing it for the first time"*

S low rain was washing out the October heat, she looked
around, and she realized she was surrounded by men
from the past. The corner table at her favorite lunch place
put her in a position to see everyone going in and out of the
restaurant. One of her favorite neighbors was coming in with
a woman who was not his newly picked fiancé. How many of
us women does he have in his life simultaneously? Someone
else she dated a few years back was sitting alone in a restaurant
across, he is always alone, fifty years of lonely life selling planes
and making sure there is nothing out of place in his model-
looking spotless apartment. And then she felt it. She looked
left to another end of the restaurant. No way! Her eyes were
fixated on a tall masculine, mountain-looking man talking to
another man she had never seen before. Ten-something years

ago, he was everything she wished for in a mate. Deep inside, she still desired him, but memories of all the numerous times she gave it a chance and not once they worked sobered up her wild romantic aspirations again. She never got over him and probably never will, but the universe has made everything possible for her not to be his. He is toxic to women kind, and no love in the world could change that, even hers. She saw his profile on Seeking too, the most dangerous arrangement anyone could enter. Being by his side was like walking on a minefield, one hand on 911 speed dial at all times.

Her lunch date kept looking at his phone. They did not have any feelings for each other except friendship. He is a great guy with a huge heart and a beautiful soul. And she let him waste her time for the second time this fall. Every time he made a mess out of his life, she coached him back from a crying lost cub to a roaring lion. He was the only male charity project she felt okay maintaining.

A year and a half ago, he wrote her on Seeking. Forty-three years old married father of five was passing by her town monthly. He was good-looking and in great shape. She never understood if he ever accomplished anything on his own or if he was solely living off his trust fund. But that did not matter because he was always nice.

And while she was time-traveling into her past romances, her lunch date was doing the same thing. He had a condition some would call "he was bewitched," others would label him as a hopeless romantic. Emotional attachments and toxic relationships even the smartest of us have difficulties dealing with experiencing for the first time. He was dealing with his first of its kind, and that's where she came into this picture because she was an expert.

A couple of years ago, this happily married, healthy, wealthy, good-looking father of five met a young twenty-something years old brunette at the airport, and from that day on, he was never the same. The girl was pretty and energetic. She had ideas, wishes, needs, and desires nonstop every second of her day. She was a legitimate escort, with the manager setting her up on her work affairs. A line of work like that affected her so deeply. Even months and months of love, financial support, trips, gifts, and promises of a greater future did not change how she felt being with this beautiful-hearted man. No matter how much he gave her, he still felt like "a lot of free work" to her. And he still wanted to do more and give more. So much more that he left his happy, stable life, wonderful wife, and five children. And the moment he told his dark-haired mistress he was all hers, she left him. And it gets tricky. Because they both did the right thing, they followed their hearts. The problem revealed itself as his realization he never had her heart, but he still wanted her back. The wound was so fresh no common sense or truth would make him change his mind.

And only looking at his heartbeaking story from the side, someone with experiences like her, could see that he only wanted to solve problems to feel important. And young brunette was the definition of the word "problem". He needed to lift drunk her off the cold bathroom floor and carry her to the bed. He needed to help her quit prostitution and gain a good normal stable job. He had a need to become more successful in order to buy her all the designer-labeled nonsense she wanted. He needed to be robbed by her relatives, hoping it would better their lives and straighten his relationship with his troubled romantic charity project. And all this could have been avoided if he did not marry such a wonderful woman as his wife, who was always happy with everything and never asked for more. If she only knew how different everything would have been if she indeed asked for more. That more he lived for, his unfulfilled desire to help, to please, to solve, and to comfort.

He is truly beautiful on the inside. And one day few months after whole a lot of domestic violence, legal battles, lawyers, courts, settlements, and other shit, his young troubled brunette found someone else. Someone troubled in similar ways as her. And they are happy now, at least for now.

And she was very happy for him, as he had no other choice than to move on.

CHAPTER 37

Cold Cold Heart

"For some astronomical number she could be simply bought or she could be unconditionally loved. And those are only ways you could have her or influence her decisions"

There was a time when she thought she came to her limits, she has been active and adventurous, but she was not meeting anyone different. Numerous exceptional men, intelligent and kind, talented and exciting, athletic and innovative, sexually advanced and not at all. Not being in love for almost a year made her wonderful life ordinary. There was nothing she was not overcoming or not accomplishing. But in the feelings and emotions department, she was not living. At this time, it was almost like she was watching her love life on a tv screen before her, but she was not really participating in it.

Some days she would make a connection on Seeking with men who were interested in her, and they were interesting to her, but they were not in the exact location or time zone as her. They would exchange little messages here and there weeks, sometimes months apart, and disconnect again. Facebook would suggest these people as possible friends to her, and she would click on their profiles to see who they were in public. And yet again, she was interested. She was very interested.

When he messaged her his dates for visiting her city, she lost track of his Seeking Arrangement profile. She remembered he was around 50 years old, tall, blond, athletic, and dreamy-looking. Single, no children, intelligent, and well-established. His Facebook and Instagram confirmed how dominant he was in his life, a combination of a love for people and an even bigger love for himself. Something was very powerful about him. She did not understand what precisely that was until months later. It was a scary thing. Sad and irreversible.

The fact that he was ready to go on a date an hour after he landed after over a four-hour flight on a workday was refreshing! She was excited. She did not know what the plan was, and she did not care. It was a pretty cold winter night, even for the paradise state she lived in. She exited the shower, slid into her favorite leather pants, and threw on a little fur jacket over a white t-shirt. This was not how she dressed but how she wanted him to see her tonight. It was her way of trying to dress down and fit into a world he was accustomed to. Classic North West was meeting fabulous South East.

Always on time, she stood in front of the hotel elevator a minute before ten. Sliding doors opened, she made two steps in and stood in front of him face-to-face, lips inches away. They looked each other in the eyes and did not talk for a whole minute on the elevator ride up. She was comfortable, and he seemed the same. She walked into his hotel room and went straight to wash her hands, ongoing pandemic set the tone for new human behavior, and she gladly adopted just a few of the new rules.

She was taking her fur jacket off and asking him how tired he was, whether they were going out for dinner, how his flight was, and how he was doing overall. He turned around from his luggage and started to walk towards her. Despite her questions, he responded, "I am not tired enough to give you a massage." She smiled, she stopped talking, she took the rest of her clothes off and layed on his bed facing down. He sat on top of her and rubbed her lower back in a way so she understood he was very familiar with his doings.

He was trying her on. He was testing himself if he wanted to touch her more, smell her, taste her. Seconds later, his mouth was exploring the back of her neck and slowly going down the spine to the end of it and the beginning of their own Fifty Shades story. If you thought Christian Grey was emotionally unavailable, wait until you meet this guy.

Hot, steamy, powerful fucking. Gentle but strong. His tongue always ensured she was ready and wanted before his pulsating dick thrust into her. It was never long or innovative enough for her to get tired or lose interest in more. Physically at the end of every intimacy, she felt like the very next stroke would shutter her spine or whole core. Mentally she was unsatisfied with the same reoccurring routine, and emotionally she was done with him. But she kept coming back. And back. And back. For a few minutes or a couple of days. It felt like something was missing, and she was trying to find it. Over and over again. She was trying to connect with him longer than for a few seconds, but he could not take it, not with time, not with care. He just could not.

Outside of fucking she could not touch him. He could not hold her hand, hug her, or endure her hugging him. It was not allowed. Never. To her, it was death in a physical state. She was not scared of it or him, she did not try to change him, but she desired more of him. And that made her stay and try to understand him.

On the second date, they went on a nice romantic dinner. He was opening doors, letting her have her hands around his waist while waiting for a table to sit down. They were a perfect-looking, perfectly behaved-couple on display for everyone to see. He said something ordinary, but it was special to her. He said, "We are the only couple here who looks like we belong together." And it slowly started to make sense to her. At least, that was she thought that night. He was not feeling. He could not. His mind and body only relied on his thoughts, unaffected by emotions. His emotions were imprisoned deep inside so long ago that it was hopeless to hope for him ever to feel anything again. So, she felt bad for him. She knew this was short and temporary, but she stayed. Because around him, she felt safe. And maybe she had a little hope for a miracle.

She would win little battles like convincing him to share a bite of his food or let her kiss him once on the shoulder or the neck after sex was over, but every time she lost that war. His castle was not possible to breach. She was always invited to come in and walk around but never touch anything unless they were fucking. That was the only time she felt like they were together.

Until it did not, his life and the events were changing. He knew he had a chance for something new, a new state, a new home, a new type of relationship, and new feelings. He was testing himself, and he was testing her. He was trying to break himself by breaking her. We all have weak spots inside, and she had two of those. For some astronomical number, she could be bought, or she could be unconditionally loved. And those are the only ways you could have her or influence her decisions.

He, on the other hand, always seemed to want to be normal. Normal was easy and boring to her. She tried that in the past, which made her very unhappy. He did not know that. He did not know many things because he was convinced he knew everything already.

Time was not changing anything. As much as she did not find a way to "alive" his emotions, he did not find ways to influence her decisions. He wanted to be with her on his terms, a married couple living in two different houses, spending not more than an hour a day together, mainly for the purpose of influencing his social status in the eyes of his clients or strictly fucking. And the night when she felt he sexually was so rough with her to the point her wrists and back were to the breaking point of an injury, she said goodbye. There was nothing she could do for him. No one could.

CHAPTER 38

Lost Inspiration

"Her goal to get to know this guy and not to piss him off before food makes it to the table was the paramount"

O nce upon a real dream!
She was thinking of a dream from the perspective of the traditional Cinderella story. A lovely girl with a loving heart had a dream, girl's dream was handed to her by a Fairy Godmother, and when it was time to make her dream a reality once and for all, she decided to run away being afraid that her true love Prince will not love her if he sees her in skimpy clothes. Let it sink in. And that is an excellent example of what not to teach little girls.

On the other hand, she was thirty-five years old, an educated, independent mature woman, and yet, a similar mistake was made.

His Seeking profile was like any other on the website, with a slight difference in net worth. A man able to make and keep over fifty million dollars in his life must, absolutely must, be more interesting as a person than another majority percentage of almost four billion males. There would be something in his mind she would die to explore and get inspired by.

By the time she finished reading his profile info, her inbox had made a cheerful noise, and she got a notification for her favorite perfume coming her way. He was old school! A Gift from her Wish List on the site. She wondered why he gifted her perfume and not flowers. Perhaps he was a bit materialistic.

Tall, extremely toned by workouts but lean body, well-groomed from head to toe, casually but tastefully dressed, straight back, and great posture! He arrived at a restaurant they picked for dinner on time and joined her at the hostess stand. She felt it right away. Power. Strong energy. Intense, cold, and scary energy surrounded him. He was a Prince In Shinning Armor on the outside and dark on the inside. But dark to what extent? This game just escalated from interesting to fascinating! It meant she had to watch every word and intonation she chose to accompany her words. Her goal to get to know this guy and not to piss him off before food made it to the table was paramount.

About the Author

Alice London was born in Eastern Europe and immigrated to the United States in 2006. She is a former professional model and a life coach. A widowed single mother living her American dream in Miami Beach (Florida) and inspiring others to achieve the same. Alice and her teenage son are avid world travelers and action sports enthusiasts. Alice is working on setting a standard for today's motivational thinking, one mind at a time. "Men of Seeking Arrangement" is her first novel.

Made in the USA
Columbia, SC
21 November 2023

56fdd4d1-142d-46d5-b47d-1dc68f64d8baR01